"You are to inherit everything, but only if you can prove within one year that you are mature enough to handle it."

"Tell me, Mr. Logan," Melanie replied, "did my uncle have any idea how a person can prove anything as intangible as maturity?"

Clay didn't look at all disturbed. "Actually, he said that the ideal proof would be for you to marry someone the executor approved of."

"I must *marry* to get my inheritance?"

Kathleen O'Brien, who lives in Florida, started out as a newspaper feature writer, but after marriage and motherhood she traded that in to work on a novel. Kathleen likes strong heroes who overcome adversity, which is probably the result of her reading all those classic novels featuring tragic heroes when she was younger. However, being a true romantic, she prefers *her* stories to end happily!

Recent titles by the same author:

BARGAIN WITH THE WIND
TRIAL BY SEDUCTION
WHEN DRAGONS DREAM

THE HUSBAND CONTRACT

BY
KATHLEEN O'BRIEN

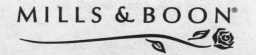

All the characters in this book have no existence outside the imagination of the author, and have no relation whatsoever to anyone bearing the same name or names. They are not even distantly inspired by any individual known or unknown to the author, and all the incidents are pure invention.

*First published in Great Britain 1998
Harlequin Mills & Boon Limited,
Eton House, 18-24 Paradise Road, Richmond, Surrey TW9 1SR*

© Kathleen O'Brien 1998

ISBN 0 263 81222 7

*Set in Times Roman 9½ on 10½ pt.
01-9811-61821 C1*

*Printed and bound in Norway
by AiT Trondheim AS, Trondheim*

CHAPTER ONE

"HEY, watch it," Clay Logan growled, reaching out to grab the shoulder of a four-foot-tall jester who had just barreled past, sideswiping him with a plume of cotton candy.

"Well, sor*ry*," the kid said defensively, frowning at the pink mess on Clay's shirt cuff. "I didn't even *see* you."

Clay plucked at the goo and tried not to look as annoyed as he felt. It wasn't easy. He had to be in court in an hour, and his shirt was ruined.

"That's okay." He summoned a smile. "Maybe you can help me. I'm looking for Melanie Browning. Do you know where she could be?"

"*Our* Miss Browning?" The jester shook his head. "She was being Juliet this morning in the play, but now..." He shrugged. "Sorry."

Clay sighed heavily as he felt the beginnings of a headache. He knew where Melanie Browning *should* have been, damn it. She should have been in his office where they'd had a ten o'clock appointment. She had baldly stood him up—no call, no excuses. And all, apparently, for the pleasure of playing Juliet at the Wakefield Boys Academy Medieval Day Fair. He rubbed one last time at his sleeve and then gave up—the stain was just spreading. Now his shirt *and* his fingers were wrecked.

Silently he cursed the benevolent impulse that had brought him here to track the woman down. He must have been insane. He should have buzzed Tracy to send in the next client and merely mailed Miss Browning a whopping bill for the missed appointment.

The jester guiltily eyed the damage he'd done. "Well, maybe I can find out for you," he offered. He turned to a pair of teens sitting on a nearby bench. "Hey—you guys know where Miss Browning is?"

One of the older boys laughed scornfully. "Why would we tell you, dork?"

Clay frowned, surprised by the gratuitous rudeness. Who were these kids? The boys, maybe fourteen or fifteen years old, were among the very few here today who were not wearing medieval costumes. Too chronically cool, no doubt, Clay thought, irritated by the swaggering boredom on their adolescent faces.

"You're not telling me. You're telling *him*," the jester said, pointing at Clay as if the presence of an adult settled the question.

The teenagers didn't seem impressed. They held their hands awkwardly behind their backs, and Clay could see two thin threads of smoke curling just over their shoulders. Smoking, at their age on school grounds? Rude *and* stupid.

"Him?" One of the boys stared at Clay, his smile defiant. "Who's he? God?"

Clay met the sneer, unimpressed himself. He knew their type. Real scary guys—except for the cowlick and the acne and an occasional unplanned octave swoop.

"Yeah, I'm God," he answered blandly. "And I'm late for the Apocalypse. So how about an answer, and I'll let you get back to your smokes. Do you know where Miss Browning is or not?"

"Nope," the boy said, his shoulders jiggling as he hurriedly stubbed out his cigarette. "We haven't got a clue."

That much was obvious, Clay thought wryly.

The jester scowled. "Well, you *did* know, Nick. You were with her after the play."

The cowlick stirred. "Yeah, well, that was *hours* ago, dork," he said. "We're not Melanie's keepers, you know."

"No—she's *your* keeper!" The jester turned to Clay with a gap-toothed grin. "You see...Nick is Miss Browning's baby brother."

Clay's interest suddenly sharpened, and he gave the cowlick a second study. This was Nick Browning? He took in the boy slowly, from the greasy, chin-length hair tucked behind his large ears, down to the huge jeans that let an inch of plaid boxers peek through. His gaze rested at the boy's feet, where he wore expensive shoes that were supposed to make him fly like an NBA superstar but undoubtedly didn't.

God, he thought, what a punk. Maybe Joshua Browning had been right to tie up the inheritance after all. Now that he'd seen Nick, Clay had to agree that no doting twenty-four-year-old big sister was likely to be up to taming this teenage terror.

Clay, on the other hand, was a thirty-one-year-old, cynical, trial-hardened lawyer who definitely did *not* have a soft spot for budding juvenile delinquents.

He gave the boy his courtroom glare. "I find it difficult to believe you don't have any idea where your sister is, Nick," he said softly. "Perhaps you'd like to think again."

Nick seemed to consider stonewalling—but only for a split second. Then, as if instinctively, he straightened his spine and let his tone slide a shade closer to courtesy. "I think...over on the softball fields," he mumbled. "At the human chess match."

"Why don't you show me?" Clay made it a polite suggestion.

As if pulled by an invisible string, Nick rose sullenly from the bench and began shuffling across the school grounds. Clay gave his helpful jester a low thumbs-up and followed the slouching teen through crowds of giggling sword swallowers, whooping javelin throwers and diminutive sceptered kings.

Nick didn't speak, so Clay was able to concentrate on avoiding the dozens of carelessly wielded weapons. He steered a particularly wide path around all cotton-candy sticks, ice-cream-cone towers and hot dogs slathered with mustard.

"This is it," Nick muttered as they reached the game fields. He tilted his head toward the chess match, which was already in progress. "Over there."

Clay scanned the players. All adults, teachers, no doubt, in full costume—black and white kings and queens, knights and bishops. He double-checked the queens but couldn't find anyone who looked much like the picture of Melanie Browning that Joshua had kept in his library. She'd been only sixteen in the photo, but she'd looked older. Long brown hair, wide blue gaze, full, sulky lips...

"Which one is Melanie?"

Nick grunted and averted his eyes. "Believe it or not, she's the white knight," he said, staring at the ground. Clay suddenly wondered whether having his older sister work at his school might embarrass the boy. "Isn't that stupid? They wanted her to be a queen, but she said knights had more fun."

At that moment, someone called out a move, and the white knight strode to the center of the board, obviously playing to the crowd with an exaggerated swagger. With a silver-gloved hand, the knight raised a long sword high in the air, apparently ready to hack some hapless black chess piece to ribbons.

The watching crowd murmured appreciatively. The May sunlight glinted on the aluminum foil of the sword's long blade, sparkled like silver fire on the sequined glove, then spilled down the knight's pristine short white tunic and tights. Clay couldn't help noticing how the costume outlined the swell at the breast, the rounded tuck of the buttocks, the graceful curve of the thigh.

For the first time this morning, his mood lifted slightly. That, he had to admit, was indisputably the sexiest medieval knight he had ever seen.

Suddenly the knight's sword dropped comically. From behind the helmet came a feminine voice that was both melodic and annoyed as hell. "Hey—wait just a minute! Where's the black knight?"

The knight's free hand reached up to yank off the silver helmet, and a cascade of thick chestnut hair spilled onto slim, tunic-clad shoulders. God, Clay thought with a strange inner lurch, Melanie Browning didn't look older than her age. She looked younger, as innocent and wide-eyed as if she were a student herself.

She shook her head in laughing disgust. "For Pete's sake, how am I going to kill the man if he isn't even *here*?" She propped her helmet against her hip and scowled at the chess master. "Wasn't Dr. Bates the black knight?"

"He probably forgot," someone called out, laughing.

"You know philosophy profs," someone else chimed in. "He's probably still at home deciding whether to be or not to be."

Melanie's blue eyes sparkled, though she obviously tried not to smile. "Well, we *have* to have a black knight," she insisted. Her gaze swept the crowd, found her brother. "Nick! You always wear black. You'd be a perfect kni—"

"No way," Nick said emphatically, backing up. "I'm outta here. I just brought this guy—" he jerked his chin toward Clay "—to see you."

Melanie frowned slightly at Nick's rude tone, but her smile returned as soon as she saw Clay's suit. *Wow*, he thought irrelevantly. What a smile!

"Oh, yes, perfect!" Grinning, she pointed her sword triumphantly at Clay. "You can be the Dark Gray knight. That's close enough." She extended her hand, silver sequins sparkling. "Good sir, would you be so kind as to step onto the chessboard so that I may run you through?"

Clay couldn't help returning the smile, which surprised him. He was still irked that she had stood him up—and he definitely didn't have time for this foolishness. But, sensing that the match was about to be salvaged, the crowd began to clap. Someone handed him a crude, thick wooden sword painted black, and wrapping his fist around the grip, he stepped onto the square in front of Melanie Browning.

She had put her helmet back on, hiding all that glorious hair. It should have rendered her androgynous, but Clay had never seen anything more distinctly female.

"You must be Mr. Gilchrist," Melanie said as she bent forward into a fighting stance. She smiled sweetly inside her helmet and touched his sword with hers. "I'm so pleased you've already met Nick," she said, beginning to parry lightly. "He's not exactly excited about taking tennis lessons, but I'm sure you'll bring him around. He's a good kid, and he's got a talent for tennis, I think."

Clay met her thrusts, careful not to bend her elegant aluminum-foil sword with his clunky wooden one. "I'm afraid you've mistaken me for someone else," he said. He was surprised to see that she had a natural grace and handled her sword as if she'd taken lessons. Could she really be that awkward boy's sister? "I'm not a tennis instructor."

Her sword paused a moment, but she began fighting again quickly. "You're not?" She backed up a step. "But you were with Nick, and I thought..." She tilted her head, laughing at her mistake unselfconsciously. "Nick always says I have a bad habit of jumping to conclusions. Rats! I just hate it when he's right."

That probably didn't happen very often, Clay thought, but he found himself reluctant to voice the words. Her tone was full of tolerant affection. Tennis lessons, indeed. From Clay's observation, the kid could make better use of a drill sergeant.

"Oh! What was I thinking? I know who you are!" With a flourish, Melanie drew a circle in the air with the tip of her sword—a useless but flashy maneuver—and the crowd roared appreciatively. Obviously, Clay noted, the gregarious Miss Browning was beloved by all members of the Wakefield Boys Academy—most of whom, *not* coincidentally, were male. "You're the math tutor, of course! I should have known by the suit. You're Mr.—"

Clay shook his head.

She hesitated. "The baseball coach?"

Clay sighed. This could take all day. "No," he said firmly.

She laughed, unchastened. "Well, now that we know who you're *not*, I'll just hush up and let you tell me who you *are*."

"My name is Clay Logan." Somehow he kept his voice neutral. "I'm a lawyer. I'm handling your uncle Joshua's estate."

The laughter died on her full lips, the smile dropping like a kite deprived of wind. She knew the name—there was no doubt about that. She froze in her position. Behind the home-made helmet, her blue eyes narrowed, fixed unblinkingly on his face.

"Clay Logan." She spoke the name in a dark monotone. Slowly she extended her sword, and with deliberate paces she came forward until the glinting silver tip grazed his shirt, right over his heart. "*You're* Clay Logan?"

"Yes." He glanced at the sword. "Is this where you're supposed to kill me?"

She didn't laugh. She didn't even move. Her arm was perfectly steady, the point unwavering. He let her hold that stance for a long thirty seconds. Out of his peripheral vision he could still see the crowd laughing and munching on candy apples, but he could no longer hear them. He heard only her heavy, agitated breathing, saw how it made her breasts strain against the tunic. He had no doubt that, if her sword had been real, she would have run him through on the spot.

Her instinctive antagonism wasn't personal, of course—when she'd believed he was the tennis pro, she had been all smiles. No, this smoldering resentment was directed at her uncle's lawyer. She had hated her uncle, and apparently that contempt spilled over onto anyone who had been his ally.

And, God help him, she didn't even know about the terms of the will yet. If she despised Clay already, what would she do when she learned the details, when she heard about the nasty little clause Joshua had insisted on inserting?

Suddenly Clay wished himself anywhere but here. What had he been thinking? Had he really believed he could soften the blow by delivering the terms of Joshua's will face-to-face? Had he really thought that she would appreciate the personal touch? What a fool he'd been! If ever two people were *destined* to be enemies...

The crowd was growing restless, but she showed no signs of moving. Finally, with a strange reluctance, Clay lifted his own sword and slowly applied pressure to hers. The sparkling aluminum foil bent easily under his crude black blade, curving into an impotent droop that pointed only at the ground.

She looked at the ruined sword for a moment, then, tossing it onto the grass, she raised her angry eyes to his. "I was supposed to capture you," she said tensely. "You were supposed to die. You've spoiled the match."

"I'm afraid," he said slowly, "that I'm about to spoil a lot more than that."

Her elbows propped behind her on the picnic table, Melanie sat backward on the bench, staring out through the dappled branches of the overhanging magnolia and deciding that sometimes life was just too ironic to bear.

She could see Clay Logan out of the corner of her eye. He was buying two snow cones from a diaphanously garbed princess in a heart-shaped headdress. The princess seemed to be enjoying the transaction immensely. She had offered him extra syrup three times.

Not that Melanie could exactly blame her. For a moment, back when she had mistaken Clay for Mr. Gilchrist, Melanie had been a little dazzled herself. She had taken one look at those aquiline features, those springing waves of rich brown hair and broad, elegant shoulders, and she had instantly begun debating whether it would be bad parenting to date Nick's tennis instructor.

Yes, darned ironic, Melanie repeated to herself, pretending not to watch. This gorgeous human being was Clay Logan. Wouldn't you just know it?

He didn't even look like a lawyer. In spite of his twentieth-century power suit, he had the air of a knight who would bring his lady treasures, a chest heaped high with golden coins and rubies as big as his fist. Or at least one ruby. Was that too much to ask? One twenty-five-carat, heart-shaped ruby that had been in her family for a hundred years. The beautiful, infamous Romeo Ruby.

But that, of course, was the final irony. Clay Logan wasn't bringing her anything but a slap in the face from good old Uncle Joshua. *I'm afraid that I'm about to spoil a lot more than that*, Clay had said, but she had known it before he spoke. Joshua had disowned her eight years ago. Why should the tyrant have changed his mind on his deathbed?

No, her uncle hadn't left her a penny. All that remained now was to find out how this slick lawyer, Clay Logan, had worded it. She closed her eyes against the bright May sunlight. How exactly does a lawyer justify robbing someone of her birthright?

And how was she going to manage without it?

"Here you go." The picnic bench rocked slightly as Clay

settled his weight on it. She opened her eyes and stared at the cup in the outstretched hand as if she hadn't ever seen such a thing before. "You wanted a snow cone?" he repeated patiently.

No, she hadn't. She had been trying to buy a little time to collect her composure. His showing up like this had been oddly unsettling. All that robust masculinity and suave confidence... Industrial-strength machismo was a rarity on a boys'-school campus.

And then there was the way he had turned her lovely sword into a piece of overcooked silver spaghetti—don't tell *her* that wasn't a deliberate power play. He knew that she had needed this inheritance desperately, and he was warning her that there was no way she could fight her uncle's will—or the lawyer who had drawn it up.

A sudden stinging behind her eyes startled her. *No, damn it.* She wouldn't give in to weakness now. She wasn't the type to whimper and beg. She straightened her spine. So what if his sword was bigger than hers? When he informed her that she was disinherited, she intended to laugh in his movie-star face.

"Melanie? Do you want this?" He sounded irritated, as if he had begun to suspect he was dealing with a simpleton. She took the paper cup, glancing at his shirtsleeve as she did.

Suddenly she frowned. What was that? That pink blob... surely he wasn't wearing a pink polka-dot shirt? That would be a cute sight in a courtroom. The image pleased her. She felt a satisfying urge to chuckle.

He seemed to sense her amusement. "Cotton candy," he said, turning over his wrist so she could see the extent of the damage. "Insidious stuff. I can't get rid of it."

"Suck on it," she said. She raised her gaze to his, enjoying the surprised furrowing of his brow. She blinked innocently.

"I beg your pardon?"

"Suck on it," she repeated sweetly. "You do know how, don't you? It's easy. Just put your lips over the stain and—"

"Yes," he interrupted, "I think I remember how it works."

She raised her brows, daring him, knowing, of course, that

it would be miles beneath his dignity. But hey—she could play power games, too.

To her amazement, he shrugged slightly, slipping his jacket free of one broad shoulder, then the other. He folded the expensive coat, laid it over the picnic table and then, watching her the whole time, he slowly raised his wrist to his mouth.

He was going to do it. *Oh, heavens...* She hadn't noticed before what a sensual mouth he had, but there was no missing it now. *Oh, my...* A generous mouth, lips full but hard-edged, as if they had been laser-cut into the perfect shape.

Damn. She had meant to throw him off balance, but now, like a fool, she was the one blushing. Oh, Lord, wouldn't she ever learn to squelch these hotheaded impulses? She should have known one little off-color word wouldn't embarrass a man like this.

She couldn't quite take her eyes off those lips. A tiny wriggle of discomfort moved in the pit of her stomach as he lowered them over the stain and covered it. She held her breath and waited. His lips were almost motionless. Only a subtle rhythmic pulse at the corner of his jaw hinted at his mission, but that pulse seemed suddenly to beat in time with her blood.

Inhaling a stiff breath, she lifted her gaze. He was still watching her. His brown eyes were flecked with gold, the irises deepening to dark chocolate over the pure white of his sleeve. She opened her mouth to say something, anything. Preferably something lightly sarcastic—that was her specialty. If she could only think of something.

But her mind was on strike. Before she could come up with a single witty syllable, he was finished. He lowered his arm and, without exhibiting the slightest interest in the results of his labors, smiled at her enigmatically.

"Interesting," he said. "It's not as sweet as you'd think, is it? A lot of things are like that. They look quite innocent, but—"

"Mr. Logan," she broke in tersely, holding her snow cone so tightly that blue syrup trickled over her fingers, "why don't you get to the point? You didn't come all the way out here today to swap laundry tips."

"No." Still smiling, he leaned back against the table, getting comfortable. He obviously knew that their symbolic tussle for superiority was over, and he had drawn first blood. He flicked a glance at her fingers. Blue blood. "I came because you missed our appointment this morning. I wondered why."

She stared at him. "We didn't have an appointment."

"My secretary seems to think we did." He propped his snow cone in a crack of the table. "She set it up a week ago. She said she confirmed it yesterday afternoon."

Melanie ran her clean hand through her hair. This was crazy. She couldn't have forgotten a call from her uncle's lawyer—she had been praying for that call every time the telephone rang the past two weeks.

"There's some mistake," she said. "I wasn't even at home yesterday afternoon."

He lifted one eyebrow. "What about your brother?"

Something in his tone made her feel defensive. "Well, yes, Nick was there, but he certainly wouldn't ever have—" She broke off self-consciously. Of course Nick would have. He was dreadful about messages. But Clay Logan couldn't have known that. Why would he, after seeing Nick the grand total of about two minutes, automatically assume it was all the boy's fault?

But she knew why. Because Clay Logan had no patience for teenage boys, especially troubled ones like Nick, that was why. The smoothly groomed attorney in front of her had undoubtedly never slipped one foot off the fast track from cradle to college. He'd probably been president of his preschool.

"Well, whatever happened, I'm sorry about the mix-up," she said, hoping he'd let it drop. "Would you like to reschedule?"

"We could." Clay hadn't moved from his half-reclining position. He looked completely comfortable out here at the picnic grounds in spite of his regimental-striped tie and wing tips. "Or I could just tell you the terms of the will right now."

She caught her breath. So it was that simple, was it? Obviously it wasn't going to require reams of paperwork and notarized signatures to tell her what Joshua Browning had left her. One word would do it: Nothing. He had left everything to charity, just as he warned her he would on that awful night eight years ago.

She wondered numbly whether Clay would even say he was sorry. Or did he, perhaps, think this was what she deserved? She could only guess what Joshua had told his lawyer about his wild, ungrateful niece.

"Okay." She put her snow cone down carefully, then met his gaze. "Now is fine."

"Good." But Clay didn't speak right away. His gaze drifted to the next picnic table, where Dutch Allingham and Josh Smithers were forcing bewildered beetles to race down the length of their swords.

The silence stretched. She tried to ignore it, concentrating on wiping her hand with paper napkins. But she noticed that Clay's forefinger flicked against his thumb, the only sign of perturbation she'd seen in him yet. Perhaps, she thought, he did regret, just a little, what he had to say.

"Toward the end of his life, your uncle insisted on drafting a rather strange new will," he said slowly, returning his gaze to Melanie's face. "I hope you'll take time to think it over carefully before you react. I know it's going to come as a shock."

She laughed, and the sound was harsher than she had intended. The boys looked up from their beetle race and stared. "I doubt it. I knew my uncle very well."

"So did I."

"Did you really?" She eyed him coldly. "Did you live with him for eight years, dependent on him for every scrap of food you ate, every stitch of clothing you wore, every smile, every hug, every bit of affection you received?"

"No." He frowned. "Of course not."

"Then I don't believe you knew him quite well enough," she said. "Otherwise there wouldn't be a single controlling, vindictive thing he could do to surprise you."

Clay sighed. "Look, Melanie, I'm sorry..."

His voice sounded genuinely regretful, and even that little hint of pity threatened to destroy her hard-won composure.

Bracing herself, she dug her heels into the sand beneath the table and narrowed her eyes.

"Violins aren't necessary, Mr. Logan. I've known since I was sixteen years old that my uncle planned to disinherit me."

One side of Clay's mouth—that wide, generous mouth—quirked up. "And you never let yourself hope that Joshua might change his mind?"

"Never," she lied, though she could see that he knew it wasn't true. "Never."

"Then perhaps I'm going to have the pleasure of surprising you after all." Clay crossed one leg over the other and propped his head against the palm of his hand. He was the picture of languorous ease—darn him. Melanie's own posture was so tight she could almost hear her muscles humming.

"Well, you can try," she said, managing what she hoped was a lazy smile, but which felt annoyingly like a sickly one.

"Okay." He smiled. "Two months before he died, your uncle established what is commonly known as an incentive trust. In that trust, he left everything—his house, his collection of antique maps, his stocks, bonds and cash holdings and, of course, the Browning ruby—to one person." He eyed her, obviously assessing the impact of his list. "That's an estate totaling well over twelve million dollars."

"Left them to—" she swallowed "—to whom?"

Clay twitched one long, lazy forefinger toward Melanie. "To you."

For a long moment, she didn't respond. She couldn't. Her vocal cords had gone slack. Everything? Even the ruby? That wasn't possible. Joshua had said—

"There are certain conditions, of course."

Melanie's numb hands slowly clenched into fists in her lap. Conditions. Of course. Nothing Joshua Browning had ever offered in his life had been unconditional.

"That," she said, "might have been predicted."

"Yes, perhaps. But I did warn you. This is where it gets strange." Clay leaned forward. The sudden movement stirred the air, and the trembling breath she took tasted sickly sweet, like overblown magnolias. "It's true," he said. "You are to inherit everything, every single penny, but only *if* you can, within one year, prove that you are mature enough to handle it.''

She stared. ''Prove *what*?''

Clay shrugged. ''Apparently Joshua had certain...reservations about some of your life choices. And, as well, he feared that your brother might coerce you into doing something unwise.''

''Nick would?'' Her lips twisted. ''What? Did Joshua think I might cut up the Romeo Ruby and use it to buy my brother video games?''

Clay didn't smile. ''Or private schools. Designer shoes. Tennis lessons.''

''Twelve million is a lot of tennis lessons,'' she snapped.

''Yes, it is,'' he answered calmly. ''Too many. I think that was Joshua's point.''

She stared at him. How dare he take that superior tone? This was so utterly preposterous, and yet how like Joshua it was! Though Clay made it all sound so pragmatic, Melanie knew that Joshua hadn't cared a fig what became of the money. He'd just wanted another way to control her, even from beyond the grave.

''Tell me, Mr. Logan. Did my uncle have any idea how a person can prove anything as intangible as good judgment? Surely maturity can't be quantified.''

Clay didn't look at all disturbed by her bitterness. ''Actually Joshua suggested several ways. He thought a review of your finances might help, combined with a look at Nick's grades, interviews with his teachers, things like that. But in addition he said that, in his opinion, the ideal proof would be for you to marry someone the executor approved of. Someone who couldn't be suspected of marrying you for your inheritance.''

Marry her for the money... Had Joshua really said that? Had he really still needed to throw that in her face? Memories of that long-ago night, of an elopement that failed, a love that was proven false, flooded over Melanie like a river of shame.

''Oh, that's rich! I must *marry* to get my inheritance? For

God's sake! That's...that's..." Realizing she was in danger of sputtering, she took a breath. "That's positively feudal."

Clay nodded gravely. "So I told Joshua. But he was adamant."

Suddenly she longed to tell Joshua exactly what she thought of his "incentive trust". But it was too late. She would never again tell Joshua anything. He was dead. For the first time, it seemed to sink in that her long battle with him was over.

And this...this *insult* had been his parting message to her.

She stood up though her legs were shaking. She couldn't listen to another word. Tucking her cardboard helmet under her elbow, she threw her head back, tossing her hair behind her shoulders. She had expected to be hurt, but *this*... This was worse than anything she had imagined.

"Listen carefully, Mr. Logan," she said, enunciating each word clearly. "I want you to tell my uncle's executor, whoever this paragon might be, that I intend to claim my inheritance. The Romeo Ruby belonged to my parents. When they died, my uncle took everything that should have come to us—"

"Their wills named him as beneficiary," Clay interjected reasonably.

"Perhaps," she said coldly, "but they meant for him to look after it *for us*. I'm quite sure it never occurred to my parents that my uncle would try to disinherit Nick and me."

He waited, not contradicting her. How could he? He must know it was true.

"So you tell my uncle's executor that I expected something like this. Tell him I've already hired a lawyer, and he's going to break this will." She narrowed her eyes. "Tell him that I'm *not* going to lower myself to prove anything to anyone, especially not to any man who'd participate in such a contemptible charade as this."

Clay was smiling, a strangely charming, lopsided grin that created a small dimple where his cheek met his jaw. She scowled at him. What the devil was so funny?

"I mean it, Mr. Logan. If a snake like that thinks he can actually pass judgment on *my* life, my decisions, my maturity..."

Her words faltered as a sudden suspicion settled cold and thick in her stomach. She folded her arms across her waist and tried not to shiver.

"All right, I'll bite. Why the smile? Who's the executor? Just who is low enough to be my uncle's accomplice in this farce?"

Clay tilted his head. A ray of sunlight fingered its way through the trees and struck golden highlights into his hair. He was still smiling, his cheek still dimpling.

"I'm sorry, Melanie," he said quietly. "It's me."

CHAPTER TWO

"OH, BLAST all!" Melanie balefully eyed the charred bread sticks on the pan in front of her. "Just look at this," she said, raising her voice so that it could be heard in the adjacent living room. "I burned them. Damn that man!"

Ted Martin, who was spread out comfortably on her sofa watching a basketball game on television, lifted his blond head. "Who?"

"Clay Logan, of course. Who else?" She picked up one of the blackened twists, which was the consistency of a hockey stick, and knocked it against the counter.

It felt perversely gratifying to hit something. Today had been a very, very bad day. Only forty-eight hours after receiving a copy of Joshua Browning's will, Melanie's lawyer had called this afternoon with the tragic news. However medieval it might seem, the will appeared to be ironclad. Clay Logan was too good to have left any loopholes.

Her lawyer had been sympathetic, but the bottom line was that he just couldn't agree to take the case on a contingency basis—the odds of winning were too slim. His best advice, he said, was that she should negotiate with Logan, who was by all accounts a tough lawyer but a fair and just human being.

Well, not by *all* accounts. If anyone had asked *her*, the report would have been a great deal less flattering. She wasn't ready to agree he was a human being at all.

She whacked the bread stick one last time. "Damn, damn, damn the man. May his grandchildren be cross-eyed. May all his dogs have fleas."

With a resigned sigh, Ted sat up and turned off the television. "Why? Logan didn't make you burn the bread, did he?"

She came to the doorway, scowling. "Of course he did."

"How?" Ted ambled into the kitchen and extracted a fat

21

strawberry from the pie on the windowsill. "Did he break in and sabotage the oven thermostat?"

"He might as well have." Melanie pulled the strawberry from his fingers just an inch short of his lips. "Honestly, Ted, you're as bad as Nick." She tucked the berry back into its cradle of whipped cream. "Now, where was I? Oh, yes—I curse Clay Logan and all his dogs because he's an insufferable man, and I hate him. I'm so busy hating him, in fact, that I've ruined a perfectly good dinner."

"No, you didn't. The spaghetti's fine. And I made one hell of a salad. Let's eat."

She wrinkled her nose. "I can't. I hate Logan too much to eat."

"Good. More for me." Ted reached around her to rummage for utensils. "But seriously, are you sure it's Logan you're mad at, Mel? He was just the hired gun, wasn't he? The will itself is your problem—and that was your uncle's idea."

"Yeah, I suppose so." She knew Ted was right, but her annoyance was no less intense for being irrational. She could still see how Logan had looked at the chess match the other day, sizing her up, obviously deciding that Joshua had been right. "But I wish you could have seen his face when he told me. He was the hired gun all right, and he thoroughly enjoyed pulling the trigger."

"Well, that dirty rat!" Ted's attempt at a gangster accent failed miserably. "I'll stab him in the alley like the dog he is." He tossed silverware nosily. "Or I would if I could find a damn knife."

Melanie patted his forearm affectionately. Good old Ted—she thanked heaven for his support this past year. It had been a tough year for both of them. Ted's fiancée had left him last summer, a break that had wounded him more deeply than he liked to acknowledge. And at about the same time, Melanie's life had been turned upside down by the arrival of her little brother, who had decided he could no longer tolerate living with his domineering Uncle Joshua.

Melanie herself had escaped Uncle Joshua's tyranny years ago, running away when she was only sixteen, but Nick had stayed with the old man until last year, when their relationship finally grew so stormy that the boy had sought sanctuary with Melanie.

As the dean of boys at Wakefield, Ted had heard about Nick's change of address immediately and phoned Melanie for a conference. Since then, Ted had become her best friend. She'd rested her woes on his shoulders a hundred times.

And nice shoulders they were, too—trim and solid and warm. She wondered, not for the first time, why their relationship had never blossomed into a romance. Perhaps Ted wasn't over Sheila yet—Melanie suspected he might never forget his former fiancée. But Melanie didn't mind. In spite of Ted's many charms, she had never felt anything more than friendship toward him. No leap of flame. Not even a tiny wriggle of heat.

The sad truth was, she'd felt more sexual awareness watching Clay Logan launder his shirt with his lips today than she ever had here in Ted Martin's arms.

Yes, life was just a charming little bundle of ironies, wasn't it?

Still, his big brother comfort was just what she needed now, when her heart was so sore. Who would have guessed she would find her uncle's death so unnerving? Was it possible she had been harboring hopes of an eventual reconciliation?

Surely not. She might be naive, immature, impractical—all the things Joshua had accused her of—but she wasn't a complete idiot. She'd given up yearning for his love years ago. Now she merely wanted justice.

Still—suddenly she couldn't bear the memories of her uncle. Joshua, bent over his dusty old maps. Joshua, barking into his cellular telephone. Joshua studying the financial pages. Joshua, completely ignoring the little girl waiting in the doorway.

She caught her breath, stunned by the wave of sorrow that overwhelmed her. Instantly aware, Ted dropped the flatware and wrapped his arms around her gently.

"It's okay," he said, his voice low and steady. "It's going to be okay."

"I know." She shut her eyes. Ted was right. Everything

would work out, love or no love, money or no money. Somehow she and Nick would get through.

"Oh, man, that is so gross."

Straightening, she looked up to see Nick squatting by the open door of the refrigerator, scrounging irritably through the bowls and bottles.

"What's gross?" With a smile, she patted Ted's cheek, extricated herself and hurried to her brother's side. She peered in at the shelves. "Has something spoiled?"

Nick grimaced and grabbed a cold leg of fried chicken. "Yeah, my appetite," he said. He stood up, gnawing on the drumstick. "People can see you two through the window, you know. Can't you save that crap for when I'm gone?"

Melanie slowly closed the refrigerator door before speaking. She hardly knew which transgression to address first. "Don't use that word, Nick," she began.

But he merely grunted and turned his back to her. He had the remote control in his hand and he flicked on the television.

"And what do you mean, when you're gone?" she asked, keeping her voice neutral. "Were you planning to go out? It's a school night, you know. It's Tuesday."

"Wow." Nick didn't turn around. "News flash. It's Tuesday."

Behind her, Melanie felt Ted's tension snap. She touched his arm, warning him, but it was too late. "Listen, Nick," he said in the tone he ordinarily reserved for the Wakefield campus, "that's no way to treat—"

Nick finally looked around. His face was hard, closed in. "Hey, we're not at school now, okay?" He tossed the stripped chicken bone toward the trash can. It missed by two inches, landing with a disagreeable splat on the linoleum. "You're not the dean when you're *here*, man."

"Nick! Apologize to Mr. Martin immediately," Melanie ordered, but her words were almost lost beneath a sudden barrage of honking. Five short, aggressive, obviously impatient blares reverberated into the living room.

The sounds acted on Nick like a starting pistol on a sprinter.

He yanked his grimy baseball cap from the kitchen table and darted for the door.

"Nick." Melanie's voice was unyielding.

The boy paused. She could almost see him working to swallow his pride.

Finally he turned to Ted. "Sorry, Mr. Martin," he said, dragging every syllable out with effort. "I guess I lost my cool there. I really didn't mean to be so rude."

Ted still looked ruffled, but he accepted the apology fairly graciously. Melanie breathed a sigh of relief. One more crisis averted. Life with a teenager was like this—all peaks and valleys. Poor Nick seemed to be strapped to a hormonal tiger—and Melanie was whipping along behind, holding the bucking tail, trying to hang on.

"Sorry I was being a pig, Mel," he said, turning to his sister with an expression so angelic she almost laughed out loud. Who did he think he was kidding? "Figgy and I were going out for a burger. His brother Bash is driving. We'll be back by nine. Okay?"

"Oh, don't give me that sad-puppy look, you scamp," she said, reaching out to touch his dark chestnut hair, so wild and messy, yet so like her own. It was hard to stay angry with Nick. Perhaps it was because she remembered all too well her own defiance at fifteen. Or maybe it was because she and Nick had no one but each other now. "I guess it's okay," she said, "assuming you've done all your home—"

But Nick didn't dawdle an instant beyond the "okay." He was already bolting across the front yard, leaping the small iron gate and racing toward the waiting car.

Melanie followed him out, and even after the roaring muffler faded to silence, she lingered on the porch. In a few seconds, she heard Ted's footsteps. She tossed him an apologetic smile over her shoulder. "Sorry he was such a creep," she said. "Must have been a spike in the hormone current."

Ted chuckled. "If only they'd hurry up and invent a cure for adolescence."

She sighed her heartfelt agreement, but she didn't pursue the subject. Nick was gone, taking his raging hormones with him, and she didn't feel like worrying anymore tonight. Instead she breathed deeply, savoring the peace of the sweet late-spring evening. Crickets scratched, maples rustled, and in the distance a dog proclaimed himself lord of all he surveyed.

Wrapping her hand around the front post, Melanie gazed down the narrow street, studying the small, cinder-block houses. In spite of a few questionable neighbors, occasional raucous late-night fights in the house next door, she liked this cozy, unpretentious neighborhood, spotty grass, barking dogs and all. She'd take it over the sterile grandeur of Cartouche Court, Joshua's personal monument to vulgarity, any day.

"Nick hates it here," she said suddenly. Ted stirred, but he didn't jump in with a response. She liked that about Ted. He was a good listener. "Every day when we get in the car to go home, he starts singing. *Heigh-ho, heigh-ho, it's home to the ghetto we go.*" Though technically it wasn't funny, she had to smile, remembering. "It's too awful. He does it in this simply spine-tingling falsetto."

"Jeez. That brat really needs a boot in the rear, doesn't he?"

She shook her head helplessly, still grinning. "I guess he just lived too long with my uncle. Cartouche Court can kind of distort your perspective."

Ted hesitated a moment, and when he spoke, his tone was only half-teasing. "All right, out with it, Mel. Is this your way of telling me you're going to go after the inheritance after all? What are you going to do—wed some pillar of the community just so you can restore Nick to the elegance of the Court?"

She tilted a glance up into his kind, intelligent face. Darn. He read her too well. She hadn't even been sure herself, until just moments ago, what she was going to do.

"A 'pillar of the community'? Ugh. Sounds like the statue in the town square." She shivered. "No. I'd never go that far, even for Nick. But surely there's a way to get our inheritance without resorting to *marriage*."

"Oh, yeah? How?"

She hoisted herself up on the porch railing, settling her flow-ered skirt primly around her knees. "Well..." She drew the syllable out, stalling. "Perhaps I can persuade this executioner—"

"Executor."

"Whatever." She folded her hands in her lap. "Persuade this Logan fellow that I'm not quite the hopeless flake Joshua said I was." She smiled. "I mean, I do pay my bills, keep a clean house and floss twice a day. I haven't shot anyone lately, and I don't think anybody knows about that time I double-parked outside the Saveway."

Ted's brown gaze remained skeptical. "Yeah, it *sounds* easy. But the one thing you're not factoring in is your—"

"My pride?" She raised her chin. "I may be a bit...independent, but believe it or not, I can humble myself. Occasionally, anyhow." She bit her lip. "Temporarily."

"Actually it's not your pride I'm worried about. It's...well, to put it frankly, your *temper*." He lifted a finger to silence her indignant protest. "Come on, you know it would make you crazy to let Logan paw through your receipts, deciding whether you paid too much for spaghetti sauce or underwear. You're just not the type of woman who submits to nonsense like this."

She scowled. His speech had the irritating ring of truth. "You could be wrong, you know," she said haughtily. "You're the dean of boys, not the Freud of females."

"Yeah, I *could* be wrong. But I'm not." He tugged on her ponytail, grinning. "I don't know exactly what *would* make you surrender yourself to Clay Logan's authority—or any other man's for that matter—but I know what *won't*. Twelve million dollars won't."

But five hours later, when the police called to tell her that Figgy, Bash and Nick were down at the police station, she discovered that Ted was wrong.

Twelve million dollars would.

The weather was gloomy all that Saturday morning. It never quite rained, but the sky was bad-tempered, growling and spitting irritably from the time Melanie woke up until the moment

she parked her tiny sedan in the circular driveway of
Cartouche Court.

She sat for a moment after turning off the ignition, listening
to the crackles and snaps of the old engine as it settled. The
noises got weirder every day. Hooking her hands over the
steering wheel, she peered up at the mansion. She hadn't been
here in years, but the place looked depressingly the same. Big
and boxy, ugly and unwelcoming. She felt a sudden urge to
start the engine and go home.

Why was she being such a wimp? She wasn't an eight-year-
old orphan anymore. Climbing out of the car, she adjusted her
calf-length navy blue skirt, did a quick button check, then used
a forefinger to chase any stray lipstick back within the lines.
Everything was where it belonged, she decided—except her
heart, which was exhibiting a regrettable tendency to beat
rather high in her throat.

She slowly ascended the marble front steps and rang the
bell. While she waited, she studied the pseudo-Grecian statues
that flanked the double front doors. She'd always found them
disturbing—two naked, armless females who appeared to have
been frozen midflight as they tried to escape the house.
Probably Uncle Joshua's definition of the perfect woman,
Melanie thought. Mute, helpless and hopelessly trapped.

"Morning, ladies," she said, patting the truncated shoulder
of the nearest statue. "I'm back, you see. I thought I had
gotten away, but apparently it's not that easy." She wrinkled
her nose. "I guess I don't have to tell *you* about that."

Suddenly the front door swung open, and Melanie's mouth
went embarrassingly slack. For a minute, it was as if the past
sixteen years had never even existed. In spite of her grown-
up clothes, in spite of the lipstick and the car keys, Melanie
was eight years old again, staring up into the sourest face she
had ever seen.

"Mrs. Hilliard." Her voice even sounded like a child's. She
cleared her throat, swallowed, then tried again. "It's good to
see you, Mrs. Hilliard. How have you been?"

The woman's long, square jaw tightened, and her black
eyes, surrounded by dark smudges below and thick, slashing

black brows above, narrowed. "I've been missing your uncle, that's how I've been," Mrs. Hilliard said flatly. "I don't suppose you can say the same."

If her life had been a children's book, Melanie thought, like *The Secret Garden* or *Pollyanna*, Joshua's housekeeper would have been rosy cheeked and cheerful, always ready to comfort the new little orphan with a hug, or a licorice twist, or a bracing bit of country wisdom. Instead, she had been like *this*. Cold, critical and painfully candid.

Melanie's instincts told her she'd better establish new ground rules. She clamped her jaw shut, straightened to her full five-four and met the woman's gaze straight on. "I believe Mr. Logan is expecting me, Mrs. Hilliard," she said firmly, ignoring the woman's question. And why shouldn't she? It was a rude and nosy question.

The housekeeper blinked twice, then stood back, holding the door wide. "He's in the library," she said, her tone falling short of courtesy, but, at least for the moment, smothering the open hostility. After all, there was the off chance that Melanie might be able to claim her inheritance. Melanie hadn't ever contended that Mrs. Hilliard was stupid. Just mean.

The housekeeper left her to find her own way to the library, which was at the extreme end of the entry hall—a hall that by itself was almost as big as her whole house in Sewage Basin Heights.

But something was different today.... She looked toward the curving central staircase and finally realized that two workmen were kneeling on the steps, pulling up the carpet. They talked softly in some melodic foreign language, and one of them even whistled while he worked. Their chatter paused as she passed, and they smiled at her.

She smiled back, grateful for the sense of life and energy that their presence lent to the house, which was usually as silent as a crypt. During Uncle Joshua's reign, workmen never whistled.

Oh, how painfully vivid the memories were—how miserable she had been here! She felt her resolve hardening and quickened her steps. She *deserved* this inheritance, by God. Joshua *owed* her something for all those lonely years.

When she finally reached it, the dark-paneled library door was tightly shut, just as it had always been in her uncle's day. She considered barging in, but old habits died hard. So she knocked, but she knocked briskly, determined to arrive with confidence.

"Damn, damn, damn! Who the hell is that?"

They were her uncle's words. Joshua always cursed whenever the phone rang or a knock sounded at the door. Antisocial by nature and by habit, he always assumed that any contact from the outside world would be a nuisance.

Melanie put out one hand to steady herself on the paneling, but then she remembered. Not her uncle, of course not. It must be Copernicus. How could she have forgotten Copernicus? Her uncle's parrot, a bird as ill-tempered as its owner, had been uncannily precocious about picking up swearwords. His talents had delighted Joshua, who had taught him to be profane in six languages.

"Who is it? Who the hell is it?" The parrot was still posing the question querulously when Clay Logan opened the heavy door. The library within was dim. Though its domed ceiling rose to a huge skylight in the center, on a rainy day nothing but gloom came through. All that mahogany paneling was positively funereal—so it took her a moment to realize he was holding a magnifying glass in one hand and a map in the other.

He waved her in with the map hand. "Melanie. Come in. I'm just finishing up here, but for God's sake, come show yourself to Copernicus before he has a stroke."

"He won't have a stroke," she assured him, her tone slightly acid. "He thrives on irascibility. Just like my uncle."

But she walked over to the old parrot anyway and presented herself in front of his perch. She had been sixteen the last time she saw Copernicus. The bird was silent as if he'd recognized her but couldn't believe his eyes. He shifted from foot to foot and bobbed nervously, watching her through first one eye and then the other.

"Good Lord, he's speechless." Clay had retreated to the

big carved desk in the middle of the room, but he'd looked up from the map he'd been studying and was observing their interplay curiously. "That's a first."

"Oh, he'll recover. He'll be swearing at me in Portuguese pretty soon."

Clay chuckled and went back to his perusal of the map before him. Looking at him, Melanie felt a strange confusion in the pit of her stomach. He had explained that he was staying at Cartouche Court for a while, appraising her uncle's antique map collection, but somehow actually seeing him behind that desk was a shock. Joshua had spent so many hours there, bent over those same maps.

And yet Clay couldn't have looked less like her uncle. Joshua's interest in the collection had been dry, brittle, precise. The only emotion they evoked in him was greed.

In contrast, Clay seemed to be all vibrant masculinity even in repose. With his shirtsleeves rolled back to his elbows and his aristocratic profile bent over the mottled paper, he seemed excited by the map, more like an explorer than an academic. A ship's captain, perhaps, or a warring king studying the charts that would lead him to some new, exotic adventure, some thrilling conquest.

Melanie mentally shook herself. What nonsensical fancy was this? Clay Logan might have walked into her life as a black knight, but he was just an ordinary man, nothing more, nothing less. The fact that her uncle had given him so much power over her future was making her imagine things.

Striving for a more natural air, she strolled toward the desk and stole a peek over his shoulder. The map was very old, its colorful pictures quite strange and beautiful. Ships and sea monsters lurked in the oceans; heraldic emblems decorated the borders, while in each corner a face with puffed cheeks blew the four winds toward the land.

"It's fourteenth century," Clay said. He ran a long forefinger across the youthful, garlanded head of Zephyrus, the west wind. "Hand colored. Beautiful, but not terribly accurate. I would have hated to try to use it to actually get anywhere."

She looked again. "Well, at least it warns you where *not* to go. It shows quite clearly where the monsters are."

"True." Leaning back, Clay gazed up at her thoughtfully. "The only problem is that they were wrong. The most terrifying monster on this map swims in what's now the best fishing water around the Bahamas." He smiled. "Like many people, mapmakers created monsters out of their own ignorance. Out of their own fears."

His smile seemed slightly wry. Did that comment carry a double meaning? Was he suggesting that she had demonized Uncle Joshua out of her own insecurity? Watchful of her temper, she chose not to address that issue.

"I can sympathize with that," she said. She hoped she sounded confident, only slightly self-effacing. "I certainly let my fears get away from me when you came to Wakefield the other day. I want to apologize for flying off the handle like that."

He was still smiling. "No apology is necessary. I expected you to find the terms of Joshua's will disagreeable. I wasn't at all surprised that you decided I was one of your monsters. How are you feeling now? Has your attorney had time to look over the will?"

"Yes," she said uncomfortably. He must know what her lawyer had said. If she still cherished any hopes of getting the will thrown out, she would never have come here. "He tells me that my uncle's will is quite legal and probably unbreakable."

"He must be an unusually ethical man, then," Clay said, sounding surprised. "A lot of lawyers would assure you it was worth a try, just so they could bill you for hundreds of hours of 'trying'."

She bit her lower lip, wondering how honest she needed to be. Completely honest, she decided unhappily. A woman mature enough to inherit twelve million dollars didn't shrink from confronting an embarrassing fact or two.

"Well, he didn't really have any incentive to mislead me. I asked him to take the case on a contingency basis. He wouldn't have earned a cent if he hadn't overturned the will." She lifted her chin. "I can't afford to contest this will frivolously, Mr. Logan."

"Then don't contest it at all," he said softly. "Your uncle wanted a will that would stand up to any challenge, and that's what I gave him." Standing, he came around the side of the desk. "Look, Melanie, I've got an idea."

His smile was warm and utterly charming, which made her instantly suspicious. Warm, charming people didn't ordinarily work well—or very long—with Joshua Browning.

"Since you've acknowledged that I'm not technically a monster," he said, his tone teasing, "why don't we start over? We'll sit down, you'll agree to call me Clay, and we'll talk this whole thing over calmly."

She nodded slowly, banishing the suspicion. This was, after all, what she had hoped would happen. Calm. Cooperative. That wasn't so hard. She could do that.

"Good. How about over here, then?" Clay gestured to a large leather sofa directly under the skylight, the most cheerful spot in a room like this. Its only drawback was that it faced a small, strange display of antique handcuffs and thumbscrews that Joshua had collected over the years. More obsession with power.

But rather than quibble with Clay's choice of seats—that was no way to start a cooperative chat—Melanie sat, settling herself at an angle to the display. If she didn't turn her head much, she couldn't even see the nasty little items.

When she leaned back, though, the sofa suddenly hissed and writhed beneath her. She leaped to her feet, startled beyond speech. A very large reddish-brown cat—so like the color of the sofa that she hadn't even seen it—was huffily rearranging himself, angry at the disruption but too lazy to get out of the way.

Clay laughed and, reaching over, dumped the fat, furry feline unceremoniously onto the floor. "Get lost, Fudge. You're in the way."

"Damn cat," the parrot complained from his perch. "Useless beast."

Melanie stared from Copernicus to the cat, then turned her

bewildered gaze to Clay. She finally found her voice. "Is that yours?"

Clay shook his head, patting the now-empty spot, encouraging her to take her seat again. "Good Lord, no. That lazy feline belonged to your uncle."

"Joshua had a *cat*?" Melanie tried to picture it. For years, she and Nick had begged their uncle for a pet, but he'd always refused. Too much hair, too much trouble. And now—this? "My uncle hated cats. He never had a cat in his life."

"I gave this one to him a year ago," Clay said mildly. "Fudge shared tuna sandwiches with him, ate them right off his plate." He eyed her speculatively. "You've been gone a long time, you know. A lot can change in eight years."

"Obviously." She sank onto the sofa, a little dizzy suddenly, slightly disoriented. She felt like the blindfolded player in that old children's game, twirled first this way and that until she had no idea which way she was facing.

It had been a mistake to come here. She should have waited until Monday, when she could have met Clay in his office. This place had too many memories, too much emotional residue. Right now, her thoughts were so off balanced that she wondered if she could even find the words to state her case.

"I think I'd better just come straight to the point," she said, her voice hardly as steady as it should be. "Nick is at a ball game with a friend, but they'll be back soon."

"Okay," he said, settling comfortably against the sofa. "I'm listening."

"Okay," she echoed. Her voice sounded hollow in her ears. "As you may have guessed, I want to talk to you about Joshua's will. I...well, I wanted you to know that, in spite of what my uncle may have told you about me, I really am not a crazy teenager anymore. I'm twenty-four. I work. I live a perfectly sensible, even frugal..."

She hesitated. His gaze was curious, polite, but somehow unnerving. This was going to be much harder than she had anticipated. And perhaps, though these were the words she'd practiced in front of the mirror, she was going at it all wrong. Even she could hear that she still sounded angry, defensive.

She started over. "I want my inheritance, Clay. I believe I deserve it, and I'm willing to do whatever is necessary to convince you of that. Anything you need—credit reports, bank accounts, work references—I'm prepared to make it all available to you."

He raised his brows. "This is a fairly dramatic turnaround, isn't it? May I ask what happened to change your mind so completely?"

She flushed. "I've already admitted I overreacted. I've given this a lot of thought since that afternoon. In fact, I've thought of almost nothing else. I've realized that I have nothing to hide, nothing to fear from an inspection of my finances or my lifestyle." She tried to smile. "You just reminded me that a lot can change in eight years. You're right. Perhaps my uncle changed—I don't know. But I do know that I changed, a lot. In fact, if you'll give me a fair chance, you'll discover that I'm a very different person from the headstrong girl my uncle remembered."

That much was certainly true, she thought, aware of how bitter the words tasted in her mouth. The old Melanie could never have spoken such conciliatory sentences, not for a *hundred* million dollars. Even now, if it wasn't for Nick, she might happily have suggested that Mr. Clay Logan take the damn Romeo Ruby and—

"I'd like nothing better than to discover just that," he said. She had to admit he handled his victory well—his smile wasn't the least big smug. "I believe Joshua wanted you to have his estate if you were ready to handle it. It would please me to be able to turn it over to you." He leaned forward. "I'll have my secretary send you a list of everything I'll need first thing Monday morning. We can get started right away."

But she didn't stand. She couldn't allow him to dismiss her—not yet. Her needs were more urgent than she had let on.

"How long do you think it will take?" she asked, trying to sound calm, unharried. "I mean, for you to complete your...evaluation and make a decision?"

He frowned. "I don't know. It depends on what I find. As you know, the will stipulates that you have twelve months in which to prove that you should inherit. I can't imagine that it could possibly take that long." He tilted his head, studying her face. "Why—is there some urgency?"

"Yes," she said uncomfortably, plucking at the buttons that quilted the leather of the sofa. "You see, I really need to move—to get out of the house I'm in."

"Are you behind in your payments?"

She colored again. "No, no, of course not. I don't get 'behind' in my payments. It's just that I need to get into a better neighborhood—a safer neighborhood. I'll sell my house, of course, but I'm afraid that will take too long. We need to move very soon."

Uh-oh. She was babbling, not outlining the measured logic of a sensible young woman. This wasn't how it had sounded in front of the mirror. But then, the mirror hadn't given her that skeptical look.

"Right now? What's the rush?"

"It's Nick," she said miserably. Clay's eyes changed. Of course it was Nick, his disappointed gaze said. But she refused to let herself get defensive. "It's just that I'm afraid he's falling in with a bad crowd."

Clay leaned back, raising one brow. "If you think you can find a neighborhood that's immune to 'bad crowds', I'm afraid you're searching for an Eden that doesn't exist."

Suddenly Melanie felt something warm and furry against her calf. Fudge apparently wanted to make friends. She dropped her hand onto his silky fur and softly scratched. At least it allowed her to avoid Clay's too-perceptive eyes.

"I know, but...well, Nick's given up his old friends from school. Our circumstances are rather limited, as you may already know, so he just doesn't feel like one of them anymore. It's destroyed his self-esteem."

"What has? Not being rich? The boy can't respect himself just because he no longer lives at Cartouche Court? Didn't he know that, when he left your uncle's custody, he left the goodies behind, too? The status address, weekly allowance, the credit lines at all the best stores..."

She flushed. "You make it sound like the worst kind of snobbery."

"Isn't it?"

"No, it isn't." She heard herself getting angry, but she couldn't help it. "You don't understand. You don't realize how tough a private boys' school can be. The students are—well, it's ruthless if you can't keep up."

"On the contrary," he said, "I know exactly what it's like." Clay gave her another of those wry smiles. "I went to a private school, too. Four long years as a scholarship student. It's no fun, but it's survivable."

She stared at him, finding the concept strangely jarring. She tried to picture Clay Logan at fourteen or fifteen. Even harder, she tried to picture him ever feeling at a disadvantage. Was it possible that this man had ever been racked with insecurity, rejected by the rich boys, forced to seek companionship with near delinquents?

No. It was *not* possible—he had too much inner strength. Granted, she didn't know him very well, but his personal pride was evident in the way he carried himself. The perfect square of his shoulders, the firm set of his angular jaw, the no-nonsense expression in his intelligent eyes, were all the proof she needed. If Clay Logan had been shunned because he possessed more brains than bank account, he would simply have pitied his critics and comfortably spent the four years alone.

So how could she admit to him that Nick wasn't made of such stern stuff? That Nick's ego was fragile, his self-image built on all the wrong things. Did she dare say she blamed her uncle for that, too?

"I'm sure Nick's hurting," Clay went on. "And I'm sorry for it. But leaving Joshua was Nick's own idea. He didn't like the restrictions Joshua placed on him—and he hoped you would be a more lenient guardian. It's really no surprise, is it, that there was a price to pay for his freedom? There usually is."

"Yes, but the price is too high!" She pressed her fingertips together tightly, holding her emotion in with every muscle. "He's taken up with some new kids, kids from our neighborhood. These boys are much tougher than he is. He..." She hoped she wouldn't fall apart, thinking of how Nick had looked at the police station, so young, so frightened. "He follows their lead. This week, they were caught spray-painting city hall."

Clay's brows pulled together in distaste. "Then the problem is in Nick, Melanie. Not in your address."

Frustration pressed like a fist on her chest. "I understand what you're saying. He should be stronger, I know. But I have to deal with Nick as he is, not as he *ought* to be."

His face was implacable, and suddenly she realized she was just plain tired of begging—it was so at odds with her natural temperament. She had done all she could. If Clay couldn't feel any sympathy for Nick, then she would have to find another way.

She stood jerkily, feeling like a fool. She had abased herself for nothing. "I apologize for wasting your time," she said coolly. "I had hoped that perhaps you could expedite this...this cute little *trial* my uncle cooked up. If you won't, you won't. I don't need to bore you with all the details of our personal problems."

Clay rested his head on the heel of his hand, still relaxed in spite of her tension.

"You're flying off the handle again," he pointed out.

"No, I'm just late getting home. Thanks again for—"

"If you really feel that Nick is in danger where you are," he broke in calmly, "why not move back into Cartouche Court?" He smiled at her horrified expression. "I'm serious, Melanie. Why not? Joshua's will specifically stipulates that you may live here, rent free, during the twelve-month evaluation period. Why not take advantage of his offer? Why not come home?"

Why not? A hundred thousand memories, all of them unhappy, that was why not. She looked helplessly around the library, half-expecting to see her uncle lurking in the dark corners. But the clouds had passed over—the shadows now were honey-colored.

"Come home?" she repeated hollowly. Was this home?

"Come home," Copernicus ordered in a fierce voice that was eerily like her uncle's. "Come home, damn it."

It was obviously unanimous. Even Fudge wrapped himself around her ankle, purring. She stared numbly down at the cat, wondering why she was even letting herself consider this insanity. She leaned down to pet him, stalling.

"Damn cat," Copernicus said sullenly, ruffling his feathers irritably.

Clay had stood now, too, and was studying her closely. "Why don't you at least give it some thought? It would be financially advantageous for you, and it might even, as you say, expedite the work you and I need to do together. Fewer faxes, no phone messages to go astray." He sighed. "I could even get to know Nick better."

Get to know Nick...? She realized suddenly, with a nervous tightening in her gut, what he meant. "Oh, that's right. You...you live here now, don't you?"

"Yes." He grinned, and for the first time, in the brightening sunshine, she could see the gold flecks in his brown eyes. "But I'm staying in the guest house, in case you're worried about appearances."

"Well, I would have to be, wouldn't I?" she said dryly. "Considering that my character and my judgment are now officially on trial."

He laughed as if he thought she was quite witty, but she knew it was no more than the truth. She was the defendant, and Cartouche Court was to be her jail. And Clay Logan was prosecutor, jailer, judge and jury all in one deceptively charming package. She closed her eyes. The prisoner was in big, big trouble.

CHAPTER THREE

IT WAS the wrong side of midnight. As was his habit before retiring to the guest cottage for the night, Clay strolled quietly across the upstairs hall of Cartouche Court, his body slicing through the alternating stripes of blue moonlight and black shadow as he double-checked doors and windows.

The hall was like a long, straight saber, cleaving the mansion's eight bedrooms into two sets of four. He peered into each one as he passed, assuring himself that all was in order. With so many workmen coming and going, it couldn't hurt to be careful.

It was like taking a walk through time and space. Joshua had decorated the bedrooms to reflect different nations or eras, each using an antique map as inspiration. The Chinese bedroom, then the Irish, the Crusades, the Civil War, the St. Croix... The interior of Cartouche Court was as varied as history itself.

But silent, Clay thought, standing at the top of the stairs, scanning the emptiness. Some nameless disaster might have swept all living things from the face of the earth, leaving behind only hollow suits of armor, stopped clocks, beds that no one slept in, books that no one read.

Well, all that would change tomorrow when Melanie and her brother arrived. The transformation had, in fact, already begun.

He moved to the Chinese bedroom and knuckled the door open slightly. Over the past week, the room's simple elegance had given way to a strangely delightful chaos as Melanie's things had been sent ahead to await her arrival.

He flicked on the overhead light, wondering what new nonsense had been delivered today. On Monday she'd sent a dozen boxes, which now were stacked on the Oriental carpet. Each carton was labeled in black marker, and the careless scrawl was as impractical as Melanie herself. "Odds and Ends," she'd written, or "Boring Papers."

Her clothes had come on Wednesday. Two bulging suitcases and then a half-dozen dresses in soft, feminine prints, sent loose on hangers. They surged like flower-laden waves over the red-lacquered chest in the corner.

And here was today's addition—a small, battered sound system, tangled wires and a handful of CDs littering the elegant trestle table from the ming dynasty. And on the carved rosewood tester bed, amid the richly embroidered pillows, a giant one-eyed teddy bear winked at Clay as if amused by his grand surroundings.

"She always was a messy one."

Clay looked over his shoulder, not really surprised to see that Mrs. Hilliard was awake, still roaming the halls after midnight. Since Joshua's death, the housekeeper had tended the old man's estate with an almost obsessive care.

"Mrs. Hilliard," he said, smiling, "we've got to stop meeting like this."

She didn't return his smile—she wasn't much for grinning at the best of times—but he knew she liked him anyway. Her requirements were straightforward. She liked anyone who had been Joshua Browning's friend.

Bustling past him into the room, the housekeeper swept the teddy bear off the bed and dropped it on top of the dresses. She flattened her brows into an ominous line. "Melanie never had a bit of respect for anything. Did I ever tell you how I caught her up in the hall here, bowling down ivory netsukes with a glass paperweight? A hundred years old, they were. Priceless."

Clay chuckled. She'd told him the story at least three times this week.

"Honestly, that girl drove her uncle crazy."

"I'll bet she did," he agreed, thinking of Joshua's obsession with order and control. Even for a more relaxed personality, Melanie probably wouldn't be a very soothing roommate—all that hot-blooded temper, all that restless, volatile energy. No, not soothing. But she might, he thought, be rather stimulating....

Whoa, boy. He jerked firmly on the reins of that thought. He mustn't ever, ever allow himself to think of Melanie Browning that way. She was a client, not a woman. She barely qualified as one anyhow, with her enthusiasm for swordplay, her tomboy temper and her wide, innocent blue eyes that teared up as easily as a baby's.

But then, like a fool, he thought of how she had looked in her knight's tunic, all honeyed sunshine, silver sequins and incredible curves. Something deep in his gut tightened and warmed at the mental picture, instinct overruling intellect.

All right, so she *was* a woman, damn it. She still wasn't *his* kind of woman. He'd been in love only once, right out of college, and Allison had been as different from Melanie Browning as ice was from fire. Ally had been the Grace Kelly type—calm, blond, polished and refined until she glowed like marble.

When she had died, only a month before their wedding, Clay had vowed he'd never look at a woman again. Needless to say, such wild, brokenhearted promises couldn't be kept. Now, ten years later, he looked—he even occasionally touched—but he always went for the same type. Blond, cool, collected. Would-be Allisons who would, of course, never be Allison.

But even if Melanie Browning had been Grace Kelly herself, she would have been off-limits to Clay. He could stand here till dawn listing all the ethical violations any fooling around with *her* would represent.

"And this young man who keeps bringing over her boxes," Mrs. Hilliard was continuing as she circled the room, sniffing for new transgressions. "This Ted Martin. Who is he anyway? Why is a nice young man like that playing errand boy for her?"

"Ted Martin? I didn't know about him," Clay said, curious. "Boyfriend, perhaps?" He suddenly, intensely, hoped he was right. If Melanie had a squeaky-clean fiancé at hand, it would solve all Clay's problems at once. He could satisfy his conscience, turn over the inheritance and banish all pesky thoughts of curvaceous white knights forever.

"Boyfriend?" The housekeeper snorted. "Not hers, not on your life. Melanie's taste always ran more to drummers and dropouts."

Clay raised one brow. "She was only sixteen, remember," he chided gently.

"She was old enough to know better."

"Still, maybe you should cut her some slack," he insisted. He wasn't going to let Mrs. H. destroy his dream of an easy resolution. A "nice young man" named Ted would be very helpful; an unemployed space cadet called Ringo would not. "Not many sixteen-year-old girls go around dating Nobel Prize winners."

"Maybe not. But it's one thing to flirt with one of those longhaired deadbeats when you're sixteen." Mrs. Hilliard switched off the light with a small huff. "It's something else altogether to run off in the middle of the night and marry one."

Was she doing the right thing?

Melanie had no idea whether she was about to salvage their lives or destroy them. For seven long days, her confidence had been under seige, and she had hardly slept, scarcely eaten. Doubts had raged through her mind like guerilla warriors, popping up whenever she relaxed, attacking whenever she let down her guard.

What if she was wrong? What if this whole move was folly? What if she took Nick back to Cartouche Court and then she couldn't win her inheritance? Wouldn't it be harder than ever for him to accept his fate? Or what if Clay had been right—that the problem was Nick, not their address? Would she have put them both through this for nothing? And would allowing Clay to live in close proximity to Nick really help anything? Familiarity with Nick didn't always breed respect, at least not these days.

But when Melanie woke up on Saturday morning and loaded the last of their things into her car, she felt oddly excited. For some reason, the doubts this morning were almost inaudible, like a cry heard in the distance. Today she dared to hope.

Perhaps it just was her nature to be foolishly optimistic. Or perhaps it was the day itself. As they drove, the air was sweet with the promise of summer, and the hills rolled by like mounds of emeralds. It was a magical morning, designed to sow hope in even the most barren heart.

As she turned into the lane that led to Cartouche Court, she caught her breath. But the magic held. Sunshine sparkled along the driveway like a yellow carpet strewn with topaz. Orchard orioles, hidden somewhere behind the pink blossoms of the crab apple tree, filled the air with explosive ripples of song. A pair of comical jays, apparently sent straight from Walt Disney's central casting, cavorted in the front fountain, which splashed merrily over its marble tiers.

And there, bursting from the double doors as if shot from a bow, was Mrs. Hilliard, her arms outstretched to welcome Nick home. Nick rolled his eyes, but he climbed out of the car and, to Melanie's amazement, allowed Mrs. Hilliard to hug him. Melanie watched them, the sunlight fracturing the prisms forming as her eyes grew wet without her permission. And finally the doubts were completely silenced. For the first time since their uncle's death, Nick was smiling, laughing at Mrs. Hilliard's halfhearted reprimands, stoically enduring the cheek pinching and the kisses.

Melanie suddenly felt like joining the orioles in a song. Oh, yes—she could endure coming back. She could even bear having to bow and scrape and endeavor to please Clay Logan, Executioner. She could stand anything. Nick was happy.

Picking up both overnight bags, she followed her brother through the double doors and into the marble foyer, humming something that, had she been able to carry a tune, might have been the "Ode to Joy".

The workmen were on the job again today, crouched on the staircase, their hammers rising and falling. They both looked up and, noticing her suitcases, smiled.

"One minute," the nearer man said in a melodic Jamaican

accent. He held up a handful of carpet tacks. "Not yet. One minute."

Dropping the suitcases in the corner, she waved her hand reassuringly. "That's fine," she said. "We're in no hurry. We'll wait."

Mrs. Hilliard had scurried away, to prepare the fatted calf, no doubt. Nick was at the far end of the hall, fiddling with one of the two suits of armor that guarded the library door. Melanie's stomach tightened instinctively. No one was allowed to touch those.

"Nick," she called out nervously. "Don't."

He flung a disdainful look over his shoulder. "Why not?" Without waiting for an answer, he pulled the gauntlet loose and began shoving his hand into it. "I always do."

"You do?" Melanie couldn't believe it. "Does...I mean, did Uncle Joshua know?"

Nick screwed up his face, expressing his certainty that Melanie was nuts. "Of course he knew," he said. "We used to fight every night."

Melanie was speechless. She could have said the same, she thought dryly, but her meaning would have been completely different. She watched helplessly as Nick pulled the helmets, gauntlets and swords from both suits. He came clanking across the hall and handed a set to her, grinning.

"Here, put these on. It's fun."

For a moment, she was frozen. She half expected Joshua to come storming out of the library at any second, his handsome face red with rage beneath his distinguished shock of white hair. Six feet five inches of pure fury, under which the little girl would crumble away to dust...unless she stood up to him, unless she fought back with all the courage she could find, or pretend to find.

Melanie blinked hard. Good grief. Was she going to be reduced to a terrified child every time she entered this house? No. She had always wanted to play with those swords, and by God, she was going to do it now.

The helmet was shockingly heavy and a rather tight fit. Once she squeezed it on, she had to struggle to keep her head from tipping over, clunking her chin against her breastbone. The sight was in the wrong spot, so she had to keep shoving the visor up in order to see anything at all. And the gauntlet was cumbersome, the sword unwieldy. God, how had they managed to fight in this stuff? She wouldn't have been able to move a muscle. She would have been the deadest knight on the battlefield.

Still, it was fun. When Nick came whooping toward her, sword in the air, she found her coordination and met him thrust for thrust. Up and down the hall they battled, the fiercest of enemies. The workmen ceased their work and watched, cheering the cleverest moves, applauding the nastiest insults.

Eventually Nick backed her up against the stairwell. "Say your prayers, you murdering dastard," he commanded as he slashed his sword above her head. She leaped out of the way, but the jerking motion slammed her visor shut.

"Time-out," she cried, trying to get the darn thing open again.

Nick snorted his disgust. "Murdering dastards don't get time-out, Mel," he complained. "They get their heads lopped off. Now say your prayers."

She wrenched the visor open just in time. "No, you say yours," she said, lunging toward her brother with a stumbling gait, the heavy sword almost pulling her off her feet. "If indeed you know any, you heathen cur!"

Nick neatly sidestepped, but to her horror, Melanie kept going, propelled by the weight of the enormous steel blade in her hands. She had barely managed to untangle the sword from her feet before she thudded, shoulder first, against the library door.

"Goddamn it," Copernicus screamed from within. "Who the hell is it?"

Nick began chortling irrepressibly, and even the workmen seemed to be smothering smiles behind their hammers.

"It's me," Melanie called back grumpily, massaging her shoulder, which was probably dislocated or broken or something. It hurt like mad. "And you'd better watch your tone, you moldy old vulture, because I'm *armed*."

"And dangerous, it seems." The library door opened to reveal Clay Logan, looking elegantly amused in his gray suit and tie. He glanced at her sword, then at the library door. "There wasn't really any need to storm it, you know. It wasn't locked."

She tried to lift her chin, but it wouldn't go up. The blasted helmet must have been made of lead. The only result of her efforts was that the visor banged shut again.

"I wasn't trying to get in," she said, hoping she was facing in his direction. It was like wearing a metal blindfold. "I just lost my balance."

"You were pretty unbalanced to start with, Mel," Nick chimed in, still snickering.

Melanie spun around to give her brother a dirty look, but she couldn't find him. "Darn," she said, wrestling with the visor and finally getting it up. "I hate this thing."

"Perhaps you should remove it, then," Clay said helpfully. As if that hadn't already occurred to her! "I'd be glad to assist."

"I can do it," she said huffily, tucking her sword between her knees to free her hands. But she had forgotten about the clumsy gauntlets. When she tried to lift the armor from her head, her hands merely slid noisily across the metal.

Muttering under her breath, she knelt. Resting the sword on the floor, she tried again. The helmet caught on her ears.

"Blast all," she said, beginning to perspire beneath the hot metal. Hearing a suspicious noise, she shoved open the visor and swiveled to glare at Clay. She could have sworn she saw a smile cross his lips, but he was too quick for her. He had corrected his expression into one of perfect courtesy before she could adjust her focus.

"Here," he said, "let me help." He came toward her slowly, as if she were a skittish animal he needed to catch. Then, staring right down into her eyes the whole time, he put one hand on each side of her head and gently lifted the helmet free. He grinned as she emerged. "Arise, Sir Melanie," he said solemnly, extending a palm to help her.

Rather than appear ungracious, she took it. But if there was ever a good time to fall through a hole in the floor, she thought as she touched his hard fingers, this was it. Even when she was erect, she felt like an idiot, standing there in her blue jeans, tank top and haute-couture gauntlets. Her cheeks were hot and damp, and a thick strand of hair was clinging to her forehead. Clay dragged it clear with his forefinger.

"There. Feel better now?"

God, did he have to be so tormentingly polite? Why didn't he thunder at her as Uncle Joshua undoubtedly would have? "Yes," she managed, finding it strangely difficult to meet his gaze. "Thanks."

"Dare I hope that the urge to slay someone has passed?"

She gave him a grim smile. "Except myself, you mean?" She peeled the gauntlets off as gracefully as she possibly could under the circumstances, then used her hands to smooth her wild hair. "I'm sure I don't have to tell you," she added with a sigh, "that this is hardly the kind of first impression we had hoped to make."

"Nonsense," he said generously. "I'm growing quite accustomed to it. I'm not sure I'd even recognize you without a weapon in your hands."

Damn him. He *would* make it sound as if she behaved this way on a daily basis.

"Well, anyway, we're terribly sorry we interrupted you," she said, crooking her forefinger behind her back, trying to summon Nick surreptitiously. "Aren't we, Nick?"

"Yeah, sure," Nick said indifferently. Melanie wanted to leap across the seven feet between them and throttle the kid. Just last night she had spent an hour lecturing him about the necessity of impressing Clay Logan favorably. "Suck up, you mean," he had said cynically. "Yeah, sure, I can do that."

So if he *could* do it, why the devil didn't he? And now she couldn't even kill him because Clay already had decided she was too bloodthirsty. She propped her helmet back on the suit of armor, praying it wouldn't fall off.

"Were you working on the maps?" She hoped the question sounded friendly, not like the blatant attempt to cover Nick's discourtesy that it was. "Before we interrupted?"

"Yes," he said, watching her try to slide the sword into its sheath, apparently knowing better than to help. "I've discovered something odd. Would you like to see?"

"Oh, I'd love to!" She gave him a hundred-watt smile. The sword was hanging up on something, darn it, and wouldn't go in. "Unfortunately, Nick and I need to freshen up before lunch." She turned to Nick and gave *him* a hundred-watt glare. "Don't we?"

He shrugged. "I don't."

She shoved at the sword with repressed fury. "Of course you do. You'll want to change your clothes. You wouldn't come to lunch in *that*."

With an expression that said she'd turned lunatic, he began to contradict her. She shot lasers out of her eyes, impaling him.

"Oh." Finally he got the message. "Sure. If you say so."

The sword finally slid home. Melanie turned back to Clay, her relief so great she was afraid he could smell it. But she simply had to get some quiet time, time to regroup. Time to box Nick's ears. Maybe then, she thought, they could come back down and they could all just start over. She'd ring the bell, pretend she was just arriving.

"We'll go upstairs, then," she added unnecessarily.

"All right." Clay nodded agreeably.

"And we'll, you know, wash up."

"Fine."

She touched her shirt. "I'll change."

Clay smiled the wry smile she was beginning to hate. "Well...don't change too much," he cautioned. "Saturdays are fairly casual around here. You might as well leave your halo and wings upstairs."

CHAPTER FOUR

A COOL, thin line of sweat made its way down Clay's temple as he pounded into mile number four of his treadmill run. Only four, and already his thighs were on fire—God, he was out of shape. Ordinarily he could go an easy six without breathing hard.

But he hadn't been able to squeeze in a workout for days. Sometimes—like now, for instance—he wondered why he'd ever decided to become a lawyer. Maybe, he thought, wiping the sweat away with a forearm, he should have stuck with the life plan he'd made at ten: Buy a sloop and sail around the world with only his collie for company.

It would sure beat spending every day listening to vultures bickering over who should get Uncle Fester's stamp collection or Aunt Isadora's earrings. Take *Murphy v Murphy*—he'd been putting in sixteen hours a day all week on that one. By now, frankly, he was ready to take the whole Murphy clan out behind those Boston slums they were squabbling over and just shoot the greedy bastards.

And then there was Melanie Browning. He'd spent one whole mind-bending night trying to decipher her system of record keeping—if you could call it a system. It was really two shoe boxes stuffed with receipts, twenty unbalanced check registers and a legal pad full of stream-of-consciousness financial "planning".

Finally, two days ago, he had dumped the whole mess in a carton and dispatched it to an accountant, who might conceivably be able to make sense of it. He should hear something by early next week—assuming the horrified accountant didn't leave town.

As the odometer slipped into the sixth mile, Clay could finally feel his tension sliding away. He'd needed this. He finally stopped worrying about the Murphy mess—he even erased

Melanie's bold, careless and somehow exquisitely feminine handwriting from his mind—and gave himself up to the view.

It was worth looking at. It was actually pretty amazing.

Joshua's gym was in one of the two wings of Cartouche Court, both of which ran back from the central portion of the house, embracing the interior courtyard. Between the two wings, Joshua had built a pool. True to form, he hadn't built an ordinary Olympic rectangle. Instead, inspired by an old map, he'd constructed an Italian grotto.

Just outside the gym's sliding glass doors, a free-form pool twisted and turned through a labyrinth of mossy stone walls, cascading ferns and trickling waterfalls. At night, with artistically placed colored lamps, the effect was romantic, almost Gothic. Now, in the late, bright afternoon, the water was clean and inviting, turquoise where it met the sunlight, silvered with shadows when it fingered into the caves.

Suddenly the sunlight quivered as a door opened on the opposite wing.

Clay watched, still running in place, as Nick came barging out, a sight to behold in opalescent sunglasses and baggy purple swim trunks, carrying an oversize boom box on his bare, scrawny shoulder. Setting the stereo down, he turned the volume up so high Clay could almost see the bass shaking the sliding glass doors. The boy flung himself onto a lounger and began slathering sunscreen on his hairless chest.

More movement. This time, the door from the other wing opened by inches, and Melanie came out slowly, peering up as if she feared snipers lurked on the roof. She clutched a beach towel around her shoulders like a cloak and practically tiptoed toward the loungers where her brother lay.

Clay watched with amusement, glad of the tinted windows that gave him one-way viewing. Undoubtedly she believed he was still at the office—or she wouldn't have risked exposure at all—but she still wasn't taking many chances. She perched on the side of the lounger, hands folded in her lap, a convent schoolgirl ready for inspection. She probably even thought she was dressed for the part. She wore a one-piece white tank suit that was technically modest enough for a nun. Nonetheless, it outlined her body as clearly as if it had been a coat of paint. He felt his pace accelerate as if he were actually going somewhere.

He wondered how long her demure act could hold. Nick cannonballed into the pool, sending up a geyser that sprayed within inches of her, but she didn't retaliate. Even when he entreated her to join him and aimed his plastic water pistol her way, she merely shook her head sweetly. Within minutes, though, she was clearly restless. Her foot began tapping to Nick's rock music, and pulling the cloth band out of her ponytail, she toyed with it, wrapping her fingers in it, nibbling on it, stretching it into tortured shapes. She leaned back, sat up, lay down again. She sighed heavily.

Clay looked at his watch. Maybe another sixty seconds, he thought, grinning.

No wonder she had always been a tomboy, Melanie reflected, drumming her fingers rapidly against the lounger's armrest. Being a lady was a crashing bore.

She squinted irritably toward Nick, who was over in the deep end, dying with a great deal of fuss, apparently cut down in the prime of his life by a laser from the Planet Hellstar. He was thrashing and clutching his heart in agony. He was having a ball.

She shut her eyes against the temptation of the rippling blue water. But Nick's boom box was playing her favorite dance song—it made her hips ache to try to hold them still. And she did love to swim....

Oh, to heck with this! She stood suddenly and kicked off her sandals as if the need to be free had blown a hole right through her good intentions. But darn it, even if Clay returned home unexpectedly, he couldn't contend that being wet was a mortal sin.

Nick greeted her entry into the deliciously heated pool with a whoop of delight. "Yes! Reinforcements!" He tossed her his water pistol. "Cover me!"

He was so cute when he was like this, she thought, ducking down to let the water lap over her shoulders. The sassy punk disappeared, and the little boy she remembered returned, making her heart squeeze in her chest.

"Okay, go for it." Chuckling indulgently, she aimed the gun at the far side of the pool, quite prepared to shoot. No rotten alien from Planet Hellstar was going to hurt her little brother, not on her watch.

Nick climbed the rocks stealthily, then, crouching, made his way to the other side, maintaining the weird, squatting posture as though dodging dozens of alien lasers.

"Trouble at two o'clock!" he called, pointing to the edge of the rocks, where a fern shivered in the breeze. Melanie pivoted, pointed and pulled the trigger. A stream of water shot an arc clear across the pool, stopping the alien in his tracks.

Except that it wasn't an alien. It was Clay Logan. He was wearing only a pair of navy blue swim trunks, and the water she'd just pelted him with was sparkling in the sunlight, trapped in the crisp, dark brown hair that dusted his bare chest.

"Hi," he said, smiling pleasantly. "Having fun?"

He darted just one brief glance at Melanie's water pistol, which she had lowered in instinctive dismay. But he didn't make any comment on it. That was generous of him, she thought as she loosened her fingers and let the gun sink to the bottom of the pool. No evidence, no crime; that was her motto.

"Whoops." Nick straightened sheepishly. "Sorry about that. We thought you were the evil emperor from the Planet Hellstar."

"Hey, no problem." Clay shrugged easily, giving Nick a pat on the shoulder and a man-to-man wink. "Lots of people make that mistake."

Melanie grinned, but deep inside she had to disagree. Not today they wouldn't. Not when he was smiling like that, with the late-afternoon sun gilding his broad shoulders, casting bronze shadows just under the firmly sculpted pectoral muscles. Not when he was so full of comfortable charm, apparently aimed entirely at making friends with a fifteen-year-old scamp who, judging from his dopey grin, would be eating right out of Clay's hand pretty soon.

They began discussing some war movie Melanie hadn't ever

heard of. Boy talk—F-14s and Mach fives and sound effects. She climbed out of the pool, grabbed her towel and watched from a comfortable distance.

What a fascinating contrast they provided. Beside Clay's golden virility, poor Nick seemed all skin and bones, all awkward angles and acne. She wondered, suddenly awestruck, at the mysterious alchemy that could take raw material as unpromising as a teenage boy and fashion it into a form as poetic and powerful as Clay Logan.

The meeting of the Testosterone Club seemed to be breaking up. To her surprise, Nick wandered over to his boom box and turned the volume down. Voluntarily.

"Hey, Clay." Nick squatted on the edge of the lounger, rubbing his hair with his beach towel. "Is it okay if I bring Copernicus out?"

"Sure," Clay said. "He's in the library. Just don't drip on the books."

Nick didn't even take offense at that. He loped happily toward the house, leaving Melanie to wonder what safe subject she could find to fill her time alone with Clay. She could hardly tell him she'd been thinking what a lovely specimen of manhood he was....

But luck was with her. Just as Nick exited, Mrs. Hilliard entered, a large package under her arm and the Jamaican handyman trotting along in her wake. Honestly, it was like Grand Central Station, Melanie thought, trying to adjust to the new Cartouche Court.

"Well." Mrs. Hilliard stopped short. She sniffed. "Sorry to interrupt your *little party*," she said, making the words a reprimand. "But Denny must replace the board."

Clay slapped hands with the workman, then smiled at the housekeeper. "That's all right, Mrs. H. The more the merrier. In fact, why don't you get your suit and join us?"

Her scowl deepened brows dipping so low Melanie could hardly see her eyes.

"I've got work to do," Mrs. Hilliard said, but her voice wasn't quite as fierce as her face. "If I waste the afternoon out here, who'll be in there fixing dinner?"

Clay put his arm around the housekeeper. "Nobody. I know a magic word, you see." He leaned close enough to whisper. "Try it, Mrs. H. Say 'pizza'."

The older woman recoiled. "Anyone who brings that slop into Cartouche Court will do it over my dead body." She unwrapped Clay's offending arm and thrust the package toward his bare chest. "Here—this came for you. I hope it's bad news."

As the door slammed shut behind the woman's stiff, thin body, Denny and Clay exchanged twinkling glances. Then, with another smile for Melanie, the handyman ambled over to the diving board, singing softly in his lovely island accent.

"What's in the package?" She looked toward the box, which Clay was opening. "It doesn't look like bad news. It looks like a present."

"It is. A present I bought myself. Want to see?"

He held the box out, and she peered in. Maps. Lots of them. But... She looked closer, confused. Though she was hardly an expert, she knew that these maps were not valuable. They were brand-new and absurdly simple, merely colorful outlines of various countries that might have been useful in fifth-grade geography.

"You bought these?" She lifted her gaze. "Why?"

"All in the cause of science," he said, quickly shuffling through the set, pulling out two or three maps and setting them aside. "Remember I told you that I'd discovered something odd? Well, I want to test my theory."

"Button your face, pinhead! You're giving me a goddamn headache!"

What on earth...? Melanie turned at the strident command, bewildered. Nick, who had just arrived on the patio, was trying to hold back a grin as Copernicus, riding his hand like a king on a throne, continued to deliver a tirade at full volume.

As Nick approached the pool, Copernicus spread his wings, lifted up from the boy's hand and fluttered irritably to his T-perch, only a few feet from the diving board.

"Button your face!" he screamed again, turning his flashing eyes toward the hapless handyman, who had been using a chisel to pry up the metal base of the board. Denny's hammer froze in midair. It looked like he wasn't sure whether "button your face" could actually be parrot talk for "stop hammering".

Apparently it was. Temporarily placated, Copernicus side-stepped across his perch, ready to bring the others into line, too, if necessary.

His gaze lit on Melanie—and instantly the flash subsided. He had obviously been well trained to recognize a swimsuit. In a laughable about-face, he sidled over to her and whistled lewdly. "Ummm, sweet!" he murmured. "Sweet, sweet, sweet!"

"Oh, shut up, Copernicus," Melanie said, turning her back to the parrot. He continued to whistle the traditional construction-site come-on. "If you ignore him, he'll stop it," she said tightly to Clay. "You were going to show me something?"

"Right. Watch carefully." He held the map of Italy squarely in front of the bird's perch. "Copernicus." He commanded the bird's attention. "What's this?"

Copernicus stared silently for a moment. Suddenly he bobbed his head and let out a triumphant squawk. "Hoist the anchor, mates," he cried. "We're off to Italy!" And then, with surprising energy, he began delivering a speech in Italian. Swearing a blue streak, no doubt. Melanie recognized one or two colorful nouns.

"He did it!" Nick seemed thrilled, as pleased with the bird's trick as if Copernicus had been his own child. "Uncle Joshua was trying to teach him to recognize maps, but Copernicus never could get it right."

"Well, he's got it right now," Clay said. "Italy's easy, but watch this." He slid his fingers to the bottom of the stack of maps and pulled out another one. Melanie frowned as he held it up—even she couldn't tell which country it was.

But Copernicus wasn't stumped for an instant.

"Hoist the anchor, mates," he said again. "We're off to Jamaica!" And again he launched into a foreign monologue.

"What the…?" Looking up from the diving board, Denny sputtered, a half shocked, half amused sound that he quickly covered with his large, callused hand. "I'm sorry," he said as they turned to him curiously. "But your bird..." He shook his head. "Your bird speaks Jamaican?"

Clay chuckled. "So it appears. Do you have any idea what he's talking about?"

Denny squinted uncomfortably. He listened to Copernicus a moment, glanced nervously at Melanie, then ducked his head. "I'm not so sure," he said, twisting his hammer between his hands. Finally he looked up, smiling helplessly. "Maybe, I think, something about your mother."

Clay laughed out loud, the sound startling Copernicus into silence. The workman began to chuckle, too, quietly at first, then more openly. Nick lost control, as well, and from there Melanie knew it was hopeless. She laughed till tears ran down her cheeks.

Infuriated, Copernicus stared, trying to silence them with the fire in his eyes. Failing at that, he began to scream, forgetting all six of his languages in his fury. Finally he launched himself from his perch. Because he was well clipped, he couldn't attain much altitude, but even when he fluttered to the deck, he continued flapping around their knees with an outraged pride. Melanie held her breath, praying he wouldn't hurt himself.

Nick tried to calm him, but Copernicus refused to settle. He flapped into the rocky grotto, still screeching irritably, his feathers rustling as they bumped the walls. Nick followed. The noises grew more frantic—a wild fluttering, Nick's anxious voice, then cries of pain almost simultaneously from bird and boy.

"Nick!" Melanie ran forward, knowing instinctively that Nick had been bitten. Not the face, she prayed, suddenly remembering every one of Joshua's graphic lectures about the dangers of mishandling a parrot. Split lips, severed facial nerves, lost eyes...

She rounded one of the grotto's many twisting corners, and there they were. Copernicus had tangled himself in a water-volleyball net that hung along the wall. His wing feathers protruded awkwardly, caught in the loops. Nick was trying desperately to free the bird, working with one hand. The other hand he held up against his chest. Even in the shadows, Melanie could see the blood.

"Nick," she cried, coming closer, reaching for his red-tipped fingers.

"Damn it, Mel! Not me—Copernicus!" Nick snatched his hand away angrily. "Can't you see he's stuck?"

Melanie turned toward Copernicus, eager to help, but the beleaguered bird wanted no more interference. He snapped at her. She yanked her hand back, but not before he had taken her index finger in his beak and pressed down hard. For Nick's sake, she managed to swallow her instinctive cry of pain, rushing the fingertip to her own lips for soothing. No blood—the skin was bruised, but not broken.

Clay, approaching from the other direction, appeared suddenly in the fern-filled path. He paused, assessing the situation, then moved in quickly. He made low, calming sounds that seemed to include both Nick and the bird. He had something draped over his shoulder. A towel. Of course. Why hadn't she thought of that?

"Stand back," he said gently to Nick. "You know you can't do this with one hand."

"Be careful," Nick fretted, but he stepped back, deferring to the older man. Melanie thought she saw relief on the boy's face. And something that looked like trust.

Apparently that trust was well placed. Murmuring softly, Clay carefully began to free the parrot feathers one at a time. Copernicus looked wary but too tired to fight. He babbled under his breath during the whole procedure, occasionally throwing in a clicking noise or two. Behind Melanie, Nick's breath was fast, nervous. She herself was hardly breathing at all, her gaze fixed on Clay's long, gentle fingers.

Finally the feathers were clear. And then, after three slow twists of the net, Clay wrapped the towel around Copernicus and lifted him free of the tangled mess.

Nick's relief was immediate, a low cry of happiness. He lurched to Clay's side, holding out his good hand. "Here," he said eagerly, "let me take him."

Melanie threw her arm between them. "No!" She didn't think—she just followed her fear. "Don't touch him, Nick. He's dangerous."

To her utter shock, Nick wheeled around, his eyes flashing. "He is *not!*" he cried. His face was contorted, his voice full of tears and rage. "He's *not* bad!"

Melanie frowned, bewildered. What was this all about? She wasn't the one who had bitten him until he bled. "Nick," she began, "he—"

"He misses Uncle Joshua, that's all. That's why he's acting this way." Nick was fighting the indignity of weeping, but he was failing. "Uncle Joshua's dead, and Copernicus can't get over it in just a few weeks like you can!"

Melanie shook her head, shock stealing her voice. It was clear that Nick was talking about much more than a naughty parrot. She searched her heart for the right words. She wanted to tell Nick that it was okay, that she understood. But she wasn't sure she did. Coming out of the blue like this, his anger hurt. His words hurt. She hadn't know he thought such things.

Nick faced Clay with a pitiful bravado. "Now give him to me," he ordered. "I can take care of him." His face glistened with angry tear tracks.

Clay seemed to consider, then he slowly opened the towel. As if he had understood it all, Copernicus stepped obediently onto Nick's fingers.

"See?" Nick glared at Melanie. "He was just scared, that's all. He's lonely and he's scared, and that makes him do things he knows he shouldn't do. Don't you ever call him bad again."

With that, he walked away, heading toward the library with a dignity in his skinny shoulders that was somehow heartrending. She wanted to go after him, to take him in her arms, but she couldn't. He didn't want her help.

Clay touched her arm briefly. "I'll make sure he's all right," he said in a soft voice.

And then he left, too, following the sobbing, bleeding little boy into the house.

Melanie had waited out by the pool for almost an hour. Though Clay hadn't said so, she felt certain he would come back. He would understand that she needed to talk to him, that she needed to be sure Nick was all right.

The time had passed quickly. Denny finished his work and left. The sun slid farther down the horizon, like a balloon losing air. The shadows around her grew steep. Still, Melanie didn't want to leave. He would come. She slipped back into the heated pool for warmth. She would wait a little longer.

A few minutes later, the timer for the grotto lights flicked on. Romantic blue and violet beams backlit the ferns. She could clearly see the neon orange water pistol lying at the bottom of the glowing turquoise water. Finally, just when she was about to abandon hope, she heard the quiet click of a door opening. She swam to the coping and clung to it, looking up eagerly.

It was Clay. He didn't seem at all surprised to see her still out there, as if they had made an appointment. Smiling, he sat down on the deck, dangling his legs in the pool beside her. The sunset was the color of claret wine on his shoulders.

"Nick's fine," he said. "The finger looked worse than it was. We dunked it in hydrogen peroxide and then wrapped it up. He'll live."

Something inside her softened and relaxed. "Thanks," she said, "for everything."

"My pleasure," he said casually. A small silence dropped over them, settling as softly as darkness was even now falling on the patio. Melanie sensed that he was deciding whether to talk about the rest of it—about the angry things Nick had said.

She hoped he wouldn't. The words still felt raw, like a new cut. She wasn't ready to explore them, especially not with him. Something about this man made her feel wrong-footed, like a child facing the teacher whose homework she had forgotten to do.

But that wasn't really true, was it? She paddled her feet in an aimless slow motion, feeling the warm water slip under her arches, between her toes. He might make her feel ill-prepared, uncomfortable—but he didn't make her feel like a child. The truth was...in Clay Logan's presence, she felt much too much like a woman.

His thighs were just inches from her head, and she eased away, hand over hand along the coping. Her hair floated over her shoulders, a dark cloud moving in the water.

"You look like a mermaid," he said, his voice low and gently teasing. "A lonely mermaid, waiting for her sailor to return."

"Well, that makes you a sailor, I guess." She smiled at him, more comfortable now that a full foot of water separated them. "Because I was waiting for you."

He didn't answer right away. He took a deep breath, then exhaled deeply. "Funny," he said, his tone musing. "I was thinking just today that I should never have abandoned my childhood dream of sailing around the world. It was a damn nice dream. Just a boy and his dog, living on Hershey's candy bars and rainwater, sleeping under the stars, digging up chests of gold on uncharted islands."

She wished she could see his face better. He sounded half-serious. And something else was in his voice, too. Something rueful, perhaps. Something sad.

"Why didn't you?"

He shrugged. "Reality intervened. Boats have to be paid for—not to mention candy bars and shovels. I'll tell you, though, if I'd known how cute the mermaids were, I would have done it anyway."

She was silent, not sure how to respond. She liked the thought of him as a little boy, wandering with his puppy, dreaming dreams. It made him more human, less intimidating, which helped. It also made him even more attractive, which didn't.

Her grip on the coping slipped slightly, and her feet churned, searching for purchase. *Oh, Melanie, you fool.* She was in way over her head.

"I seem to remember coming out for a swim." He tilted his head. "Mind if I join you?"

Oh, dear. She swam slowly toward the edge of the grotto,

out of harm's way. "Of course not," she lied politely. "Come on in. The water's great."

He didn't bother going to the steps. He just supported himself on the coping with his arms—the corded ribbons of his shoulders and triceps shifting, tightening, until she could have mapped his musculature with heart-stopping accuracy—and slid into the pool. His body knifed neatly into the water, long, strong legs first, then the soft darkness of his trunks, and finally the V of curling hair that ran down the center of his ridged chest.

Her stomach tensed. This was ridiculous, she warned herself. And dangerous, too. Clay was her executioner, not her boyfriend. It was merely the shock, she reasoned logically, of seeing him half-naked. It wasn't anything personal. It was pure biology—the way nature had designed any woman under a hundred to respond to any man who looked even remotely like Clay Logan.

It was what assured the survival of the species.

She just hoped *she* could survive it.

He was only ten feet from her now. He ducked down and emerged five feet closer, shaking drops from his hair. She backed up, her shoulder blades crushing ferns.

He cocked his head quizzically. His lashes were long, damp and spiked. "Are you okay?"

She pried her fingers from their grip on the rock. "Sure," she said. "I guess it just feels funny to be swimming after dark. Joshua would never have allowed—"

"You know, Melanie," he said pleasantly, making slow circles with his arms, circles that seemed without any effort to bring him closer, and then closer still, "we'd probably get along better if you could remember that I am *not* your uncle."

She laughed nervously. Oh, she knew that all right. With every sensitized nerve ending along every inch of her body, she knew that.

"I'll try," she said, easing around the corner, hoping to put some distance between her tingling body and this man who was not, by any stretch of the imagination, her uncle.

The move was a mistake. The lagoon twisted, lapping into

a shadowed cove that had no other outlet. A tiny waterfall burbled softly down the rocks behind her, and the noise was sensual, wet and whispering, like lovers' kisses. Clay followed her, of course, and the small pocket of lavender water hardly seemed big enough for both of them.

They were practically invisible in here, she realized, her heart thudding, all the blood draining from her face. Why hadn't she looked where she was going? But her self-destructive impulsiveness was legendary. If there was any way to blunder into trouble, she would do it. Joshua had always said she dove off the high board first, then checked the pool for water on the way down.

And oh, there were so many ways to get in trouble with a man like this. For instance, she might find it impossible to resist the urge to touch that firm mound just over his heart. She might need to wipe that bead of pool water away from his lips. She might want to feel his warm, wet hands against her cold, shivering skin.

Or she might, if she had any brains at all, need to dive down, grab her plastic gun and shoot him dead. That would be the safer course.

"Melanie," he said softly, his voice flowing, resonating in the small hollow of their little cave. She bit her lip against the sound. Every time he moved, the water moved against her skin as if he had sent it out to touch her. "How's your finger? I thought perhaps Copernicus got a piece of you, too."

She shook her head. "No, no, that was nothing. He didn't even break the skin."

"Still... Let me look."

"Really, it's nothing." She edged back, but the rocks grazed her shoulders within seconds. There was nowhere to go. She tried to stand, but it was too deep. When her outstretched toes found the bottom, water rose against her cheeks, tickling her nose.

He was taller, though. The water barely covered his shoulders. Reaching out, he found her fingers underwater and closed his hand around them gently. "It's okay, Melanie," he said, his voice lowered to a murmur. "I only want to look."

When he slowly raised her hand out of the water, her heart sped as if he was about to discover some guilty secret she'd been hiding. But it was nothing, nothing at all. Just a little nip, a little ache, a little throbbing, that would soon go away.

Though his hands were large, so much larger than hers, he handled her as if she were made of glass. He began with her smallest finger, stroking, exploring, turning each one over individually until he came to the darkened nail on the index finger.

He ran his thumb over it very softly, testing. "Does that hurt?"

"No." Her voice was absurdly breathless. "Not at all. It just throbs a little." She wished she could pull her hand away without being rude. It didn't hurt, but the throbbing, which she had almost forgotten, had doubled under his touch, as if a new rush of warm blood had swept in on top of the old.

"Just a little?" He slid the tip gently between his thumb and forefinger, tracing its distended contours. "It's quite swollen, you know."

She began automatically to protest, but for proof he tilted her hand into the soft blue glow of the nearest spotlight.

"Oh, dear." Melanie subsided, seeing for the first time how much damage Copernicus had done. The skin of her forefinger was stretched tightly over the engorged tip, which was deep pink with trapped blood. She smiled sheepishly. "No wonder it throbs." She bit her lower lip, tuning in to the sensation. "I can feel my heartbeat in it."

"Yes." Clay was watching her over their entwined hands. His thumb pressed in just a little, not enough to hurt. "I feel it, too. It's racing."

It was. Suddenly she could barely breathe. It felt like something was swelling in the pit of her stomach, leaving no room for her lungs to expand.

"Well, of course it is. Look at me." She tried to grin, making a joke of it all. "Here I am, trapped in a deserted cove with a ruthless pirate who refuses to let go of my poor, wounded hand."

His eyes glittered in the subtly shifting light. "I don't think

I've heard you *ask* me to let go." He paused, smiling. "Is that what you want?"

She didn't answer right away. She looked down at their hands. Rivulets of water etched glistening patterns on their fingers. "I don't know," she said quietly. "I..." She fought for a deep breath. "I don't think so."

"Good." He cradled her hand against his hard, wet chest. His voice was very low. "Because I don't think I want to."

When had he come so close? A minute ago, they had been safely apart. Now, by inches, the slow undulation of the water had molded them together. She had lost her purchase on the rocks, and her fingers clung instead to his upper arm. It was too deep. Her feet scissored, searching for balance, but he slipped one leg between her knees and pulled her forward onto the firm strength of his thigh.

"Relax," he said. "I've got you."

Slowly, watching the gleaming of his dark eyes, she let her weight settle over him. Fighting the urge to clench her knees, she wondered if he felt her pulse there, too, on the trembling, vulnerable skin inside her leg.

"See? You're safe here, little mermaid."

But he was wrong. So willfully wrong. She was sinking deeper, drowning in the deep, liquid sensations of him, and he knew it. He touched her hair, fingering it away from her neck, easing it over her shoulders, then releasing it to cascade down her back. It was tormentingly sensual.

"I don't think this is helping," she murmured, tilting her head back to douse the sparkling sensations in the cool water. "It's just making my pulse beat faster."

"What should I do, then?" His voice held a note of husky laughter—the strangest, sexiest mixture of roguish drollery and heated tension. He brought her throbbing finger to his mouth and teased it over the half smile that curved his lips. "Tell me, Melanie the mermaid. Should I kiss it better?"

He was just joking, she thought unsteadily. Just playing with the words, with the feelings. While she... She had never wanted anything more.

"Yes," she said, a bright, hot point of anticipation lancing through her, thrusting her beyond the reach of common sense. "Please, Clay. Kiss me."

For a moment, she thought she glimpsed that same gleaming pinpoint of need in his eyes. And then he bent his head. Slowly, deliberately, he dragged his lips down the length of her finger, from the swollen tip to the soft pad of skin at its base.

"Clay," she said again, her voice breaking.

He buried his lips in the palm of her hand. He stayed there a long moment, letting her fingers cup and explore the wet-satin angularity of his face. His face... She shivered and shut her eyes. But even with no visual confirmation, he felt frighteningly beautiful, from the velvet flutter of lashes to the sand-papered thrust of jaw. Her fingers trembled, learning him.

Then it was his turn, his lips moving on, mapping her arm. He discovered the pulse at her wrist, claimed it with a groan. He slid to the pointed tip of her elbow, then rose again, slowly ascending the smooth slope toward her shoulder.

She could barely breathe. He was chasing tiny schools of flashing light through her veins. By the time he had traveled her neck, her throat, her chin, she was sparkling with need, murmuring it in small, hot bursts of fiery nonsense.

Finally he found her mouth. With a muted cry of relief, she rocked forward, wrapping her arms around him, holding him until not even the water could part them. His breath mingled with hers, hovering, waiting, asking. "Yes," she whispered. "Oh, yes."

He took her at her word. With a low groan in his throat, he gathered her melting body in his arms and let his lips descend onto hers. She had never known such a kiss, nothing even close. He parted her lips with a deft urgency, entering the shadows of her mouth as if he owned them. His tongue was sweet and hard, its probing both wild and tender.

Invisibly, beneath the water, he stroked her back, letting his splayed hands sink to her hips, tilting her into his bracing leg. Her knees trembled, and she breathed a sigh that he caught between his lips.

Just a kiss... But he was pulling responses from her that

she'd never known she possessed, like a magician plucking a string of rainbowed kerchiefs from his sleeve. Shivering, surging, burning. Aching until she wanted to whimper against his lips.

She could have stayed there forever, content to be little more than a kaleidoscope, twisted into ever-renewing patterns by his knowing hands. But all too soon, long before she was ready, he began to slow the pace.

His hands stilled, reducing the pressure. His thigh softened under her, pulling back. He slid his lips over hers slowly now, as if easing her back to reality. It was like floating to earth after riding a comet through the stars.

She murmured her disappointment. When he touched her eyelids with his thumbs, she opened them reluctantly. She didn't want to land. Like a child who has just discovered something too thrilling to relinquish, she wanted another ride.

He smiled down at her as if he was aware of all she felt.

"Sweet," he murmured slowly, his gaze still on her lips. "How could I have known it would be so sweet?"

She blinked, waiting. She wanted to ask for another kiss, but somehow she knew she shouldn't. "Sweet" didn't sound quite right, didn't sound as if he had been riding that same comet, windswept and blown with stardust....

"Was it?"

"Very, Melanie. Kissing you was incredibly sweet." Closing his eyes, he rubbed the bridge of his nose and sighed heavily. "But so incredibly stupid."

CHAPTER FIVE

"YOU'VE each got thirty seconds to sign on the dotted line. At the end of thirty seconds, Mrs. Murphy's offer decreases by five thousand dollars. It will drop five grand a day until you sign it." Clay swept the room with a cold gaze. "In a month, it won't be worth the paper it's written on."

Next to him, his client stirred admiringly. Jen Murphy had told him to play hardball here this morning, and she obviously believed she was getting her money's worth.

Clay glanced at his watch. "Twenty seconds."

Though she probably had no idea, the widow Murphy had chosen the perfect day to ask him to get tough. He hadn't slept at all last night—he'd been too busy raking himself over the coals. Too busy asking himself what the hell had brought on that moment of utter lunacy in the pool. Consequently, this morning his head pounded like punk-rock drums, and he had plenty of badass attitude to spare.

He definitely wasn't in the mood to play nice, and the vultures across the table obviously knew it. Slowly, with stiff fingers and resentful glares, they began to pick up their pens and scrawl their names onto the documents in front of them.

When it was finally over, the room clear, the widow turned to him with the same beautiful smile that had enchanted all three of her husbands. "My heavens, Mr. Logan," she purred, "you're very good, aren't you?"

So was she, Clay thought wryly. Boss Murphy had undoubtedly died a very happy man. And that was why Clay had represented Jennifer Barnes O'Neill Suarez Murphy in this dispute over Murphy's will without one bit of ambivalence, in spite of her predilection for lucrative serial monogamy.

Old man Murphy hadn't been of unsound mind when he rewrote his will. Far from it. In Clay's view, it was an eminently rational decision for Murphy to leave his five million dollars to Jen's limpid blue eyes and honeyed compliments, instead of to that pack of unscrupulous scoundrels that called themselves his family.

"I didn't do anything. They were ready to sign," Clay said, stacking papers. "And besides, you were generous. Not-quite-enough beats nothing-at-all every time."

She smiled, obviously already well aware of that. If he remembered correctly, she'd had to settle for not-quite-enough with Mr. Suarez five years ago.

"Still..." She touched his sleeve. "There was something in your voice this morning. Something...something dangerous, not lawyerly at all. You sounded more like a pirate giving his prisoner thirty seconds to walk the plank."

"I'm *not* a pirate, Mrs. Murphy." His smile felt forced. "To tell you the truth, that's not a comparison lawyers appreciate as a rule."

"A general, then," she suggested, her blue eyes twinkling. "Or an emperor."

God—she must do this in her sleep! He shook his head, laughing, well aware that she was just practicing. He was a full forty years and several million dollars short of meeting her requirements.

"Nope," he insisted. "Just a lawyer, wading knee-deep in paperwork and pretrial motions. Fairly boring, actually."

"Boring?" She ran a small pink-tipped tongue over her lower lip. "I wonder what your lady friends would say about that. I'll bet you have *lots* of lady friends, don't you?"

"Thousands. And they'd all say exactly the same thing."

She dimpled. "I think you're fibbing—"

"And I think, Mrs. Murphy, that you're slightly giddy." He stood, holding out his hand, knowing she would accept defeat gracefully. "Drunk with victory, no doubt." He smiled again. "Inheriting five million dollars will do that to a person."

She pouted, but finally, with a kiss on his cheek, she left. The invitation to a celebration lunch, which he suspected she'd been ready to tender, remained unspoken.

Clay watched the door close, then grabbed a Pendaflex folder and flung himself into his chair. Staring blindly at the file, he explained to himself in no uncertain terms that he was a fool. Would it have killed him to spend an hour toasting well-written wills with the widow Murphy? It might have been fun. It wasn't as if he could go home anyway, much as he needed the sleep. He couldn't risk a repeat of last night's madness.

He cursed, bending the unopened file in his clenched hands. Good God, what was the matter with him? Forget last night.

What had he been thinking? Oh, yes...he'd been building the case for taking Jen Murphy to lunch. So what if Jen had been his client? Their case was over. An hour's flirtation with her now could hardly get him brought up before the bar.

Not like that insanity last night.

He flung the file folder sidearm onto the desk, giving up the pretense of studying it. The real question wasn't why he had forestalled Jen's invitation. The *real* question was the same one that had haunted him all night long. What on earth had possessed him to kiss Melanie Browning?

He laid out his defense for an invisible jury. First and foremost, he insisted, there had been absolutely no premeditation. He'd joined her poolside with one innocent intention only— to try to put her at ease. To be friendly, to show her that he wasn't really an ogre. She'd been so ridiculously uptight ever since she arrived at Cartouche Court. It had been almost painful to think of the bubbling spring of her personality being capped so tightly.

So it had seemed like a good idea to go out and loosen things up. *You know*, he told the imaginary jury, *treat her like a little sister*.

Well, maybe, he thought, it would have helped if he'd ever *had* a little sister.

He'd certainly missed that target by a mile. After about sixty seconds, his brotherly banter had begun to sound like flirting, even to his own ears. He had found himself swimming toward her like a damn shark. He had wanted one thing: to touch her.

And what about all that embarrassing Dr. Kildare nonsense? He grimaced. Of all the sophomoric excuses for grabbing a girl's hand. *Should I kiss it better?* Good God, what an appalling lounge-lizard line *that* was!

The worst thing, though, was that, caught in the moment, he hadn't thought of it as a "line" at all. It was as if he had invented the words, had spoken them—virginal—for the first time ever, there in that little cove. Maybe that was because *she* had been so innocent herself, her reactions so intense, her emotions so unguarded. Prejudiced by Joshua's stories, Clay had assumed, when he'd first met Melanie, that her feelings ran close to the surface because she was still more child than woman.

But now he wasn't sure. Maybe, he reflected, he'd just grown jaded. Maybe he had known too many females like Jen Murphy, who simply didn't allow themselves to possess emotions that weren't particularly cost-efficient.

As he had discovered last night, Melanie was indisputably a woman. He'd learned something else, too—a discovery that had nearly done him in. He'd learned that transparent passions were sexier than purring, manipulative expertise any day.

His body tightened, remembering. She'd been terrified of him at first, or at least of the way he made her feel. The skirmish she'd fought with herself had been played out over her features as plainly as if it had been a film. Temptation, resistance, bravado, panic. And, finally, sharp desire, followed by wholehearted surrender.

Oh, yes. Sexy as hell. He wasn't sure how he had managed to stop himself from making love to her, right there in that nonsensical cove Joshua had built.

He could imagine, with painfully vivid detail, how it would have been. Her white swimsuit stripped away, sinking formlessly to the bottom of the pool. Ferns to pillow her head and violet light pouring over her passion-tightened features. Wet hands moving over wet skin. Soft, cool currents eddying around her, and his own hard, hot need driving inside her.

His fingers curled over the arms of the chair. God, how he had wanted all that.

She had been willing. For that one moment, she wouldn't have denied him anything. And, like the ruthless pirate she had teasingly accused him of being, he had wanted it all. Every secret she possessed, every fantasy she'd ever imagined, every dream she'd ever dreamed. And, of course, every intimate, untouched inch of her body.

Professional ethics, common sense, even morality, had all seemed like concepts from another planet. Why should the pirate king concern himself with such things? They were impotent against such towering desire as his.

But thank God some part of him still dwelt on that saner, wiser planet, the place where men simply didn't seduce young women who were in their power. And Melanie Browning was very much in his power. If she pleased him, she would be an extremely rich young lady. If she didn't...

What a hell of a mess! He realized it was hardly Melanie's fault. It never for a moment occurred to him to suspect that she might have been offering herself as a bribe. She'd offered herself all right, but it had been all instinct, no contrivance. In her sudden desire, she had reached for him the way she might have plucked an orchard apple to sate her hunger, sipped from a mountain stream to quench her thirst.

No. She was not a woman who would prostitute herself for anyone. Or anything. She had far too much pride and not nearly enough cunning.

But did she have the same respect for him? he wondered uncomfortably. Might she conceivably think he was corrupt enough to offer such a depraved trade?

It was an age-old transaction. Cash for kisses.

Or, in her case, rubies for sex.

Jesus. He'd skated even closer to the edge than he realized. He needed to pull back—way, way back. There would be no more kisses. But that wasn't enough. There must be no more sunset swims, either, no more flirtatious pirate-and-mermaid charades. Nothing but numbers on a page, meetings across desks. Nothing but business talks and suit-and-tie smiles.

Suddenly his secretary buzzed the intercom, breaking the brooding silence. "Mr. Logan," she said briskly, "there's a Mr. Frick here to see you. He says he's Melanie Browning's accountant."

Clay smiled grimly. Perfect. Right on cue, here came the numbers on a page. Now if only they were the *right* numbers so that he could give Melanie her money and send her home.

Before he did something *really* stupid.

Melanie, perched twelve feet high on the library ladder, plucked a leather copy of *Antigone* from the topmost shelf. She blew a puff of dust from the cover and watched it drift slowly down, caught in a shaft of sunlight from the big, arched central window. Some of the dust settled on Ted's head. He sneezed and looked up, smiling.

"Sorry." She brushed the cover, sending another shower of tiny particles floating down. "Uncle Joshua has the best library in the Berkshires, but he just wanted to own the books. He never read them."

Grimacing, Ted moved to a nearby panel, out of the line of fire. "Would you look at this?" He held up a gilt-edged volume. "This is the most beautiful copy of Milton's poetry I've ever seen." He shook his head, panning the room slowly. "God. Do you know what Wakefield could do with a collection like this?"

"Torture a few hundred teenage boys?" Melanie wrinkled her nose at Ted's offended expression. "Oh, come on, Ted," she said. "It's *Milton*, for heaven's sake."

He sighed, slipping the book back into its place. "In *my* school, Milton will be required reading." He jiggled the foot of her ladder. "They'll be required to *like* it, too."

When the ladder steadied, she climbed down carefully, trying not to trip on her loosely flowing skirt. "Well, no wonder you haven't opened your own school yet," she said. "You couldn't find a single boy who'd sign up to enjoy *Paradise Lost*, not if you combed the entire planet. Not even if you threw in Venus and Saturn." Reaching the ground safely, she tossed him a grin. "Though I hear Milton's a big hit on Mars."

Ted dropped onto the sofa, a dusty copy of Chaucer in his hands. "As a matter of fact, that's *not* why," he said irritably, opening the book and pretending to read. "I haven't opened my own school for one simple reason: I don't have the money."

She sat on the arm nearest him and tugged on his tie impatiently. "That's what banks are for, silly."

"Now you're starting to sound like Sheila," he complained. "But at least you aren't getting ready to fling my ring into my face." He cringed, feigning fear. "Are you?"

Holding up her hands to prove she wore no rings, Melanie smiled. "See? I'm unarmed," she said. "But Uncle Joshua has a neat little collection of thumbscrews over there that I might use if you get too difficult."

His answering smile was obviously forced, and Melanie was sorry she had pressed the subject. Darn that Sheila. Hadn't she realized that Ted was a wonderful man and a great teacher? Someday, somehow, he'd find a way to open his own school. Then the fickle Sheila would regret having had so little faith.

They were silent a moment, watching Copernicus as he busily tried to remove the clapper from his bell. The only sounds were the light tinkling of the toy and an occasional irritable mutter from the bird.

"You know, *you're* in a better position to start a school than I am," Ted said suddenly. "Cartouche Court would make the perfect campus."

She laughed, trying to picture herself as a prim headmistress, role model for five hundred impressionable young minds. Copernicus glared, annoyed at the interruption. But she couldn't help herself. The idea was impossible.

"I tell you what," she said. "If I actually inherit this white elephant, I'll rent it to you for a dollar, and you can turn it into anything you want."

Ted grunted. "Nonsense. You'd want to live here yourself."

"Not on your life," she said firmly. She'd never live here voluntarily. The house had been full of unhappy memories before, and now...

She glanced out the window, where the blue grotto sparkled in the sunshine. Nick and his friend, a blond, bouncy cheerleader appropriately named Sunny, were sitting on the edge of the pool, dangling their feet in the water. They looked so young and innocent. Quite a contrast to the steamy scene she'd starred in last night.

But she mustn't think about that. Clay had made it quite clear that he regretted every second of it—and that it would never be repeated. She bit her lip and tried to force the pictures from her mind.

Ted was studying the room with narrowed eyes, obviously intrigued in spite of himself. "You'd really let someone else take over this place?"

"Yep. But you'd better not count on it," she cautioned him, trying for a light tone. "After last night, I'm afraid my chances of winning the Miss Ideal Heiress award are tragically slim."

"Why? What happened? Did you pick a fight with Logan already?" He frowned. "Darn it, Mel, I warned you about your temper—"

"It wasn't that," she interrupted heatedly. But suddenly she wished she hadn't brought *this* subject up, either. Now how was she going to explain last night to Ted? She couldn't admit that she had practically thrown herself into Clay Logan's arms, that she had in one stupid moment confirmed everything Joshua had said about her. She was willful, reckless, easily led into folly by her ungoverned emotions. "It *wasn't*," she insisted, recognizing the skepticism on Ted's face. "I didn't lose my temper."

What had she lost? A night's sleep, definitely. His good opinion, perhaps. A tiny piece of her heart? *No, no, no.* She wasn't going to overdramatize things. The whole disaster had merely been a libido overload.

She cast one last look at Nick, who had jumped into the pool and was encouraging Sunny to join him by squirting water through his fist like a geyser. The girl was laughing, obviously loving every minute of it. See? People did those things every day. If Sunny kissed Nick, would the little cheerleader go all Gothic and guilt stricken?

Hardly. A kiss was, as they said, just a kiss.

"Well?" Ted was waiting. "What happened?"

"Honestly, we didn't fight. It's just that..." Melanie sighed, dropping her hand onto Ted's shoulder. "It's just that he doesn't like me, that's all."

"Who doesn't?"

She looked up, feeling the blood drain out of her face. Clay was standing at the library door. She yanked her hand away from Ted's shoulder, then cursed herself for the guilty reaction. She wasn't guilty. Why should she be guilty? She wasn't Nick's age, for God's sake. And it had merely been Ted's *shoulder*.

But she was protesting too much. How long had Clay been there?

She wasn't the only one who found Clay's silent appearance unsettling. Without a word, Ted straightened, quickly sliding his feet down to the floor. For the first time, Melanie realized that Ted had kicked off his shoes and had been lounging on the sofa as if he were back in her little apartment. Still, she mentally argued, what was wrong with that? She lifted her chin, refusing to give in to the irrational guilt.

"Who doesn't like you?" Clay repeated patiently.

"Oh...I was talking about Copernicus," she lied. "I was telling Ted that Copernicus hasn't ever been very fond of me."

Ted rose politely and walked to the doorway, hand extended, smile on his face. As he introduced himself to Clay, Melanie watched from a safe distance. It put a man at a definite disadvantage, she observed, to be padding around in his socks. Though Ted was fairly tall himself, Clay, who had the benefit of shoes, towered over him. In her frame of mind, she thought it looked deliberate.

And what exactly *was* her frame of mind? Well, if she had thought she'd recovered from last night's infatuation, she was dead wrong. She felt her heart skip slightly at the mere sight of Clay. Unreliable friends, hearts.

Still, she knew the nuances of his face so much better now. He looked a little tired, she thought. His jacket was draped over his arm, and his tie had been yanked down, the top button on his shirt undone. She watched his lips move—talking, smiling—and her heart stumbled again.

But even as her own discomfort grew, Ted's obviously diminished. Within a minute or two, he and Clay were laughing like old buddies.

Melanie managed not to sigh. *Et tu, Ted*? she muttered mentally, aware that Ted would never again fully sympathize with her situation. *But Logan seems quite nice*, he'd say. *Really, Mel. He's a great guy. So reasonable.*

Copernicus obviously resented being ignored as much as Melanie did—and he had more effective ways of expressing his discontent. Squawking loudly, he began ringing his toy bell with all the demanding energy of a spoiled toddler.

Clay chuckled. Without a hitch in his conversation, he approached the cage and, reaching in, teased his forefinger along the bird's jaw. As Melanie watched, the fool parrot instantly subsided. His eyes glazed over, and his head tilted to accommodate Clay's stroking finger.

"Well, he obviously likes *you*," Ted said, his tone admiring. Melanie wanted to strangle him. Didn't Ted realize there was something sinister about a man who could mesmerize that crotchety old parrot with just one strategically placed forefinger?

"He likes Melanie, too," Clay said, transferring his smile to her. He continued to stroke the bird, who lifted his wing shamelessly, begging to be scratched underneath the feathers. "How could he not? He's spent years in here, falling in love with her picture."

"Has he really?" Ted looked around curiously. "Where is it? I'd like to see it."

Melanie groaned. She'd already noticed that Joshua had kept the last picture he'd ever taken of her, a sentimental gesture that surprised her. It was an awful picture. Though she'd been only sixteen, she'd applied her makeup with all the delicacy of a call girl, and her sultry pout had been horribly affected. At the time, she'd thought she looked wildly mature. Now she realized she had just looked ridiculous.

"Oh, you don't want to see *that*," she protested helplessly, knowing by the gleam in Clay's eyes that nothing short of an atom bomb would keep him from pulling out the photograph. "I hate that pic—"

Too late. Clay already had the eight-by-ten embarrassment in his hands and was passing it toward Ted.

"Would you look at that!" Ted grinned. "God, Mel, how old were you here?"

"Sixteen," she admitted with a sigh.

"Sixteen? God, you look twenty-five." Ted shook his head, laughing. "I swear, Mel, you look older in this photograph than you do right now."

She felt herself flushing. "I know. I was a little heavy-handed with the eyeliner and lipstick at that age."

She looked at Clay, wondering if he had opened this subject deliberately. Perhaps he thought Ted didn't know about her past. Well, he'd soon see that she wasn't ashamed of what she'd done as Uncle Joshua always thought she should be.

"Remember, I was dating an older man at the time," she said, still staring at Clay. Her voice held a small metallic tone of defiance. "He was twenty-two. I guess I was overcompensating, trying to catch up."

Clay's expression didn't change, though his eyes watched her carefully.

Ted nodded understanding, touching the hair of the poor, deluded girl in the picture. "Of course. I remember." He didn't elaborate, as if he wasn't sure how much Clay already knew and didn't want to make a misstep.

But Melanie was ready to have it all out in the open. The episode had been merely foolish and rather sad, not wicked. Surely falling in love with the wrong man wasn't a sin so terrible that it couldn't even be discussed in polite society.

"Technically he was my husband." She squared her shoulders. "For about an hour anyway. Until Joshua arrived on the scene."

Ted cast a nervous glance toward Clay, whose face still registered only a polite interest. "So, tell me, Clay," he said quickly, "are you saying you think Copernicus developed a crush on Melanie's picture?"

Clay smiled. "He certainly has a strong reaction to it. Hold it up—you'll see."

Self-consciously, Ted lifted the frame, looking somewhat

bewildered to find himself playing show-and-tell with a bird. As he held it steadily in front of the cage, sunshine spotlighted the dark hair and red lips of the sixteen-year-old Melanie, frozen in that siren's sulk.

Copernicus stared, then began to bob up and down, his usual preface to speech. "Melanie," he said emphatically. "Melanie, Melanie, Melanie."

She bit her lower lip hard, trying to hold back an instinctive gasp. It was terribly strange to hear her name spoken by this bird, this oddly knowing creature whose voice seemed to be half inhuman, half the ghost of her uncle.

She smiled to cover her confusion. "Very good," she said. "Just like with the maps. Now this is where he adds a string of curses in Swahili, no doubt."

"Maybe," Clay said enigmatically, still watching the bird. "We'll see."

Copernicus sidestepped back and forth across his perch, obviously agitated. "Melanie," he said again, then made a few strangled sounds as if he wasn't sure what came next. "Melanie, Melanie, *jem-farr-leenk*. And then his eyes flashed—his pupils narrowing and his irises expanding. He turned his head sideways and finally let loose with another short, intense sentence.

It was no more than eight or ten words, Melanie felt sure, though she didn't recognize the language at all. He repeated the phrase two or three times rather, as though he was trying to perfect his pronunciation. And then, abruptly, he subsided. His eyes returned to normal. Lifting one foot, he began digging under his neck feathers with a curved toe, apparently indifferent to the dramatic reactions he had created in his audience.

Ted was laughing, Clay was smiling, and Melanie felt as if she had been slammed in the chest by a wrecking ball. She stood there, staring at the bird, feeling her cheeks flush miserably, listening to her heart thud against her chest.

What had he said? Most of Copernicus's vocabulary consisted of profanities and sailoresque insults, so she could safely assume it wasn't anything flattering. But knowing that her uncle had bothered to teach Copernicus to associate this sentence with *her* picture, a feat that she knew required months of work, was somehow disturbing.

Had he really resented her that much, even after all these years? She felt instinctively that, if she could hear the words in English, she would finally plumb the depth of her uncle's contempt.

Did Clay know? she wondered. But she knew she would never ask him. She couldn't bear to hear it, not from him.... And why did she need to know anyhow? Joshua was gone, and his contempt could hardly hurt her anymore. That his enmity seemed to live on, echoing in this bird's conditioned responses, was unfortunate, but ultimately unimportant. Copernicus was, after all, just a bird, not a conduit to the afterlife.

"Wow." Ted was staring at the parrot as if he'd just revealed the meaning of life. "That was spectacular. What language do you think it was? Russian? Polish?"

Clay nodded. "I thought it sounded Slavic myself."

Melanie took a deep breath and tried to smile. "Well, maybe it wasn't Swahili, but I'm sure it would make a sailor blush somewhere in this world."

She spoke in a carefully careless voice, walking away from Copernicus, hoping to find a little privacy over by the window. She needed to compose her face. Why did this stupid, cryptic insult hurt so much? Why did she care? She looked out onto the grotto, searching for a distraction, but Nick and Sunny were nowhere to be seen.

Ted was incredulous. "Well, don't you want to know? Aren't you even curious?"

She shook her head. "Why should I be? It's just some vulgar nonsense taught to a bad-tempered old bird by a bad-tempered old man." She blinked three times fast, but still the view of the grotto fractured in front of unshed tears. "I can get by just fine without learning precisely which epithet he decided I deserved—hothead, imbecile, ingrate..." She swallowed hard. "Tramp."

Ted fell mute. Melanie crushed the heavy drapes in one

painfully tight fist, unable to speak another word around the knot in her throat.

"You know," Clay observed offhandedly, breaking the awkward silence, "I knew Joshua pretty well, and I never once heard him call you any of those things."

She wheeled, ignoring the stinging behind her eyes. She calculated the distance to the door, praying the tears wouldn't fall until she and Ted could make their escape.

"Well, I heard every one of them," she said. "And a few more that would make even Copernicus blush. Believe me, Mr. Logan, I don't need any trained parrot to tell me how my uncle felt about me." Her voice was trembling. "Or any lawyer, either."

CHAPTER SIX

FOR the next week or so, Melanie was relatively happy.

Sunny and Nick were inseparable, and they often invited several other teenagers to join them at Cartouche Court, which apparently had become their headquarters for after-school sun and fun. They swam in the grotto; they went in-line skating on the front drive.

The sight of Nick smiling and surrounded by friends brought Melanie such deep, satisfied relief that she was almost able to keep her mind away from gloomy thoughts of Copernicus and his insults, Joshua and his will, or even Clay Logan and his kisses.

Most of the time anyway. Occasionally, when she watched TV in the den, which abutted the exercise room, she could hear the rhythmic pneumatic whoosh of the weights as Clay worked out. She knew exactly how he would look. Her wayward mind produced vivid pictures—his impressive body straddling the sophisticated equipment, muscles straining, shoulders gleaming with sweat.

But she wrapped her arms around her knees and refused to budge from the sofa. It was safer that way, she insisted. Why subject her notoriously spotty willpower to temptations few women could resist?

Worst of all, though, she had developed a particularly unwise habit of sitting in her window seat each night, reading. From that vantage point, she could see the light in the library window, where Clay was cataloguing the maps.

He worked very late. Sometimes it was two in the morning before the lamp went out. But she always watched as his long, graceful silhouette strolled across the grotto, passing through pools of violet light on his way to the guest house.

He never so much as glanced up at her wing, though sometimes, foolishly, she tried to will him to. What would she have

82

done, she wondered, if he had felt her thoughts, had turned to see her sitting in the window seat, her head resting on her arms, her face pale in the moonlight?

She would have ducked in mortification, that's what.

Still, she felt an irrational disappointment each time he crossed the patio without the slightest awareness of her. Only when the guest-house door had shut behind him did she return to her own bed. Her teddy bear stood guard there, ready to ward off dreams of bloodred rubies and pirate kisses.

Tonight she had vowed she wouldn't keep that stupid vigil. Sitting cross-legged on her rumpled sheets, with this week's bills spread around her in a circle, she tried to concentrate. But she was restless—and besides, it was discouraging to discover that she had spent the entire summer's budget on one pair of basketball shoes for Nick.

Eventually she wandered down the hall toward the Civil War room, where Nick's light still burned. He had a French final tomorrow, poor kid, and his new social life hadn't left much time for conjugating verbs. The door was ajar, so she felt free to enter without knocking.

Nick sat in front of his television, rocking carelessly on the back legs of a hundred-year-old, beautifully stenciled Hitchcock chair and thumbing the buttons of his video-game controller with an amazing dexterity. He obviously hadn't heard her come in. His gaze was locked on the screen, where a strange little beast hopped back and forth in a computer-generated jungle, and he wore headphones that no doubt were drilling rock and roll straight into his eardrums.

Behind him, on the four-poster bed that dated from 1860, lay his French book, which looked so pristine Melanie wondered whether it had ever been cracked all year. She peeled one of the earphones away and leaned toward him. "*Bonsoir, mon frère,*" she whispered. "How's the French coming?"

Nick almost fell out of his chair. Recovering, he pulled the headphones down onto his neck and pressed the Pause button. The video creature froze in place. He gave her a sheepish smile. "Oh, you know. *Comme ci, comme ça.*"

She wasn't impressed. Joshua had taught her that one, too.

"Well, 'so-so' isn't going to be good enough when it's just you and the blank exam papers tomorrow morning, is it?" She sat on the edge of the bed and picked up the textbook. "Maybe you should have let Sunny quiz you on some of this."

Nick rolled his eyes. "And have her think I'm a sweat? I'd rather fail."

Sighing, Melanie stared at her little brother, who still sometimes seemed like a stranger. After all, he'd lived with her only one year out of the past seven. Even his vocabulary was foreign to her.

"And what, may I ask, is a 'sweat'?"

"A grunt. A dummy." Nick spelled it out slowly, as if she were a dim-witted child. "Think about it. A sweat. Someone who has to study till he sweats."

She frowned, frustrated equally by his irrational logic and his patronizing tone. "Well, if you fail French, won't Sunny think you're a dummy anyway?"

Nick sighed. "Never mind, Mel. You don't get it." He returned to his video game.

God, teenagers were egotistical! Watching his back, she counted to ten. Had she thought she'd known everything when she was fifteen? She shifted on the quilted bedspread uncomfortably, remembering. Yes, in fact, she had believed exactly that.

Still, he needed to learn some manners. Reaching out, she yanked the video-controller cord loose from its outlet. Nick kept tapping buttons reflexively for several seconds before he realized the creature wasn't responding.

"Hey!" He swiveled, ready to complain. But apparently one look at her face persuaded him to modulate his reaction. "I guess you want me to study, huh?"

She held out the book firmly. "You got it."

He took it with only a small groan, which surprised her. She'd been prepared to argue at least another five minutes. When he actually opened the book and ruffled through the pages, she began to get suspicious. This was too easy. What, she wondered, did the little rascal want?

"Oh, yeah...there was something I was supposed to ask you

about.'' His tone was extremely casual. He didn't look up, which made Melanie's suspicions intensify tenfold. Nick always avoided eye contact when he found himself on shaky moral ground.

She waited. It must be something bad. She considered the possibilities—a conduct referral from the principal, a bad report card, a debt, a request for yet another allowance advance, an even later curfew...

''You see...'' He cleared his throat. ''It's just that...I don't suppose there's any money in the budget for summer camp, is there?''

Melanie stared. Summer camp? If she had come up with a thousand things Nick could have wanted, summer camp would not have been on the list. Summer camps were places without video games or television. Without candy and colas.

''It would really mean a lot to me, Mel.'' He had finally looked up, and the honest eagerness in his face drove a small dagger of misery into her heart. ''Everyone is going, all the guys. Sunny, too.'' He bit his lower lip. ''Carter Drake is going, that's for sure. He's been hitting on Sunny right in front of me all week. I can just imagine what he'll do when they're all off at camp together.''

''The camp is co-ed?''

Suddenly Nick's interest wasn't quite so mysterious. He nodded.

''Well,'' she asked, ''what's the name of this place?''

Melanie couldn't believe she heard those words coming out of her mouth. Aliens must have possessed her vocal cords. She had intended to say something completely different, something sympathetic but definite. Something that began with, ''I'm sorry, Nick, we just can't afford it...''

''Camp Windclimber. In North Carolina.'' With a clumsy enthusiasm, he pulled a wrinkled brochure out of his French book. She took it numbly and stared at the glossy pictures of rolling green mountains, white, frothing waterfalls, canoes paddled by good-looking young boys and girls with straight teeth as white as their polo shirts.

She opened the folds, scanning the public-relations hype, all the requisite buzzwords—*self-esteem, confidence, values, leadership, challenges.* Somewhere in all of this was the one essential fact she needed: the price.

When she found it, she almost dropped the brochure. Surely that decimal was in the wrong place. But she looked again. She looked three times. The decimal stayed put. A month at Camp Windclimber really did cost approximately the same as a heart transplant. Which she might just need if her system got another shock like this one.

"Nick, I—"

He broke in, his voice rough with emotion. "Look, Mel, I know it seems like an awful lot to ask. You've already done so much for me, just getting us back here to the Court and all. And I really do appreciate it, you know I do." He twisted the controller cord nervously around his fingers. "It's changed everything, living here again. Sunny's dad wouldn't ever have let her go out with me if I didn't." Melanie frowned, but Nick anticipated her. "I know, it's not how people should judge other people. Sunny's dad is a jerk like that—but Sunny's not, honest she isn't. She's really deep. You'd like her, Mel. She doesn't think about money at all."

Melanie doubted that. She was in a better position to calculate the probable cost of Sunny's haircut and manicure, not to mention her designer bikini. But she didn't say so. Nick's face was as earnest as she had ever seen it. She recognized that he really cared for the girl, with all the dangerous, agonizing intensity of a first love.

"Nick," she began again, hating this. Really hating it. But where on earth would she get that kind of money?

"Mel, please. Don't say no right off. Please say you'll think about it. I'll never ask for anything again. And I'll help pay for it. I'll do errands. I'll work around the house. I'll mow yards. I swear, Mel, I'll pay you back if it takes forever."

Which it would, she thought. Even if he mowed every lawn in Massachusetts, it would take a dozen summers to earn just one month at lovely Camp Windclimber.

"Please." The precise note of need in his voice might as well have been programmed by professionals to trigger her most protective instincts. She felt herself melting into a puddle of sisterly mush. "Please say you'll think it over."

She refolded the brochure slowly, with a deceptively calm air of utter fatalism, and took the textbook from his hands. "All right," she heard herself say as she opened the book. "Let's ace this French final first. Then I'll see what we can do."

Clay tightened his knuckles around the receiver. His voice tightened, too.

"I assure you the matter is being studied thoroughly," he said. "The decision will be based on the facts, Mr. Scraggs, *not* on which beneficiary pressures me the most."

Mr. Scraggs obviously didn't like the implication. Scraggs was the vice-chancellor of a college whose football program was one of the smallest contingency beneficiaries of Joshua's will. If Melanie inherited, the Fighting Pumas wouldn't be able to afford new uniforms, and Scraggs wanted Clay to understand what a tragedy that would be.

Finally, though, even Scraggs ran out of words. Clay cradled the phone with a heavy sigh. The Fighting Pumas were an annoyance, but they weren't the real problem. Much bigger, more sophisticated corporations and charities stood to inherit millions if Melanie was judged unfit. Like the National Research Foundation—now there was a formidable opponent. Their lawyers stood ready to contest his decision vigorously.

Because of that, emotion couldn't enter into it. He couldn't afford to hand the money over to Melanie just because he liked her, or because she was spunky and charming and funny and vibrant. He simply had to squelch the protective instincts that rose in him when he saw tears burn tracks down her soft cheeks. Above all, he had to forget she was so beautiful, so passionate, that she had been so warm in his arms....

He had to concentrate on the facts just as he'd promised that whining Scraggs he would. And, so far, the facts looked pretty dismal for Melanie.

The accountant, Frick, had organized the numbers, and the picture was crystal clear. When it came to indulging herself,

Melanie was frugal to the point of severity. In the twelve months she'd been supporting Nick, she'd bought only a half-dozen packages of panty hose, one pair of shoes and a few yards of cloth to make a new dress. It was ridiculously stringent. Compared to Melanie Browning, Cinderella had been a spoiled brat.

But that was only half the picture. In spite of her personal restraint, Melanie's credit-card debt had doubled in the past year. Trendy jeans and name-brand T-shirts, basketball shoes that cost enough to feed a small village for a week, video games, CDs, in-line skates, comic books, concert tickets. An endless parade of frivolous expenses.

Apparently all Nick had to do was point, and Melanie whipped out her credit card. And if she couldn't say no to in-line skates, what would she do when it came time for college, or a car? If she received this inheritance, she'd still be sewing her own clothes, but Nick would be flunking out of Princeton in a Porsche.

"Damn it, I won't have that young punk blowing twelve million dollars at the video arcade," Joshua had insisted testily when Clay had questioned the wisdom of the will. "I'm counting on you to prevent that. If she hasn't developed a spine, she can't have the money. It would ruin the both of them."

So now what was Clay supposed to do? Swiveling away from his desk, he gazed out the back window of the guest cottage. The moon was liquid, washing over the trees like milk. It was pale and pure and strangely reminiscent of the fragile skin on the inside of Melanie's arm. Like a fool, he had kissed that skin, sipped at the creamy sweetness.

And now he was supposed to be "objective"?

He rubbed his temples, applying enough pressure to hurt. God, what a mess! He wished fiercely that he was sailing in the Bahamas and that some other lawyer was here at Cartouche Court, trying not to get emotional about Melanie Browning.

Opening his eyes, he suddenly realized that a new light was playing among the trees. It definitely wasn't moonlight—it was brighter, smaller, slightly yellow. It darted and slid over branches like a living thing.

Clay rose, frowning. It seemed to be coming from the western edge of the property. If he remembered correctly, that was just about where Joshua had commissioned a tree house for Nick.

But it was after midnight, and Nick, who had finished his final exams a few days ago, was supposed to be spending the night with someone named Carter Drake. Clay vaguely remembered the Drake boy as one of the kids who'd been hanging around Cartouche Court lately, using the place like a mini-Disneyland.

He remembered the type well from his own private-school days. Smart and self-assured, hedonistic. Reckless for the fun of it. They were just the kind to sneak back here in the middle of the night to indulge a few unauthorized vices.

Clay flicked off his desk lamp and quietly let himself out the back door. If Nick and Co. were cavorting in the tree house at this hour, they damn sure weren't playing cowboys and Indians. It could be booze or cigarettes or sex, or God knew what else. But whatever it was, it was coming to a screeching halt.

Glad that he had already changed into an old pair of jeans, Clay made his way across the heavily treed lawn. With every step he grew more certain that he had been watching a flashlight dancing through the slats in the walls of the tree house. Its crazy, arrhythmic motion made him smile in spite of his annoyance. At least he could be sure it wasn't sex. Fifteen-year-old boys might not be very smooth, but they could do better than that.

He drew up to the ancient oak that housed the structure. Things were pretty quiet up there. Without a sound, he climbed the rungs that had been nailed to the tree trunk and slowly lifted the trapdoor that served as the secret entryway. Before he was more than six inches into the opening, he heard a strange, high-pitched whizzing noise just above him and felt a slight current of air shiver over his head.

A tiny metallic thunk sounded on the wall behind him, and he turned instinctively. It was a dart, its sharp point gleaming lethally in the moonlight. It must have shot just over him, burying itself into a drawing pinned to the wooden slat.

Clay squinted, trying to identify the picture. A break? Definitely wings. Feathers.

Copernicus.

A low gasp broke the silence. He returned his gaze slowly to the other side of the treehouse, where a young woman sat cross-legged on the floor, her hands covering her mouth in silent horror. Telltale pieces of paper, colored markers and unused darts littered the floor around her.

"You know,' he said conversationally, "I've already accepted the fact that you'll be the death of me someday. Really, the only questions left are when, and how painful."

"Oh, my God, I'm so sorry," Melanie blurted, groaning. "Oh, Clay...I had no idea it was you! I mean, I didn't know that anyone, not even you..." He smiled. She gave up and ground the heel of her hand against her forehead. "I'm cursed," she moaned. "I'm absolutely, forevermore, cursed! I swore I'd never let you catch me with another weapon. And now I've nearly killed you!"

He hoisted himself through the trapdoor, joining her in the interior which was, by tree-house standards, fairly sumptuous. It was only about four feet high, so he couldn't have stood, but if he angled his body corner to corner, he could have stretched out completely. Suddenly that struck him as a bad floor plan—it was likely to put ideas into a teenage boy's head. It had certainly put one in his, and he knew he was going to have a hell of a time rooting it out.

"Killed me? With that little thing? Sorry. You might have blinded me," he said reasonably, settling himself beside her, facing the makeshift dartboard, "but it would have been difficult to kill me." He tilted his head, raising one brow. "Unless... You haven't poisoned the tip, have you?"

"Of course not." She shook her head vehemently. "I didn't even know I'd see you tonight."

He chuckled. "I see. But if you *had* known..."

Smiling, she held up the last dart, its sharp metal point glinting in a moonbeam. "Killer jungle juice," she informed him in an exaggerated whisper. "Top of the line, straight from Borneo, or maybe Detroit. You wouldn't even have known what hit you."

"Instant paralysis?"

She nodded. "Followed by convulsions." She put a sympathetic hand on his arm. "Not a pretty sight."

"Then I'll be careful never to call ahead."

"Very wise." She had been holding back her laughter, trying to maintain her gangster snarl, but finally the giggles burst free—a lighthearted, unrestrained melody of delight at her own nonsense. He couldn't remember when he'd ever heard such an uninhibited noise. He listened, appreciating its natural beauty.

She stopped to catch her breath, and rummaging in the dark space between their bodies, she extricated a bottle. She held it up, still laughing weakly. And suddenly he saw where all her inhibitions had gone. Straight down the neck of a bottle of gin.

"Want some?" She didn't quite manage to pronounce the *s* correctly.

He took the bottle from her hand and held it up to the moonlight. It was half-empty. "Melanie," he said, smiling, "are you plastered?"

"I'm not sure," she answered somberly, studying the bottle as if she'd never seen it before. "But I think so." Still serious, she waggled a finger at him. "But you mustn't hold it against me. I found it up here, so I had to drink it, you see, so that Nick wouldn't." She sighed hard, leaning her head against the cedar boards. "And, of course, I did hope it would help me stop thinking about all the things that are driving me crazy."

He glanced at the opposite wall. "I take it Copernicus is one of those things."

She followed his gaze and glared muzzily at her handiwork. The cartoon bird had taken hits in both wings, but three other darts were lodged in the wall, six inches away from the picture.

"Yes, but I didn't get around to him until I'd had a lot to drink. I could hardly hold the flashlight. My aim was much better on the others."

"Others?" He plucked one of the balled-up pieces of paper

from near her knee. "Are these the others?" He carefully smoothed the paper open, revealing a huge, round...well, a round *thing* drawn in bloodred marker. He turned the page in every direction until he finally figured it out. "The Romeo Ruby, I presume?"

She nodded, a motion that would have looked wise and knowing if it hadn't gone on much too long. "Yes. I blame the ruby," she whispered confidingly, "for all my present woes."

"*All* of them?" He chose another discarded paper from the stash on the floor. "What about these other targets? Don't they share some of the blame?"

But as he began to open the wrinkled page, her hand suddenly shot out and grabbed his fingers. "No," she said, squeezing his hand as if she'd like to paralyze it. "No, really, the others are just nothing, nothing you'd want to see, that is. Just rough drafts, you know. And kind of embarrassing." She smiled wanly. "I'm really not much of an artist."

She wasn't much of a liar, either. But it would have taken an ogre to ignore the pleading in her eyes, the fear in her voice. And he wasn't an ogre, no matter what she thought. He let the paper fall, still crumpled into a tight ball.

"Okay," he said calmly. Their gazes locked over their joined hands, and he could see the moment that she realized she still held his hand. She squinted as if something hurt, then slowly closed her eyes.

But she didn't let go. She held on as if she was dizzy and needed his touch for support. Which she probably was, he reminded himself. She'd put away a lot of straight gin. Her fingers trembled slightly where they tucked around his, nestling into his palm. He stared down, marveling at the way pale fingers looked on darker skin, like moonlight falling on shadows. Vulnerable, somehow. Beautiful.

And yet he knew this was crazy. He was smarter than this. He had to pull away.

But he didn't. How could he, when her skin was so soft, so sweet and needy? A small breeze slipped in through the window of the little room, carrying her perfume toward him. It mingled with the other night scents, the fragrant aroma of the cedar planks, the dark, loamy dampness of the earth, the sharp, clean hint of alcohol on her breath.

They sat in silence a few minutes, listening to the wind as it murmured through the leaves. Shifting against the swaying branches, the tree house made low, creaking noises, like the wooden mast of an old sailboat.

"You know," she said suddenly, "that darn ruby has caused trouble for the Brownings for a hundred years now." Melanie's eyes were open again, and they glimmered in the half-light.

"Really?" He smiled at her. "How so?"

"Well, it began back in the 1800s, when the first Joshua Browning brought the ruby home from India. He was a heartless old miser whose daughter had monumentally disappointed him by being..." She pursed her lips, seemingly annoyed that the perfect word eluded her. "Being less than... Looking a little..."

"Ugly?"

She scowled at him. "Plain. Matilda was just a little plain." But then her nose wrinkled as if she was fighting an inner battle with honesty. "Though that giant wart didn't really help, of course."

"No, probably not." Somehow he kept a straight face.

"Okay, so maybe she was ugly. But looks aren't everything, you know." She sighed. "Anyway, when someone wanted to marry Matilda, Joshua just assumed the fellow must be a fortune hunter. Then her fiancé was abducted. The kidnappers demanded the ruby as ransom. They said they'd kill the young man if Joshua didn't pay."

"But naturally, he wouldn't."

"Hey." She peered at him suspiciously. "Do you already know this story?"

He smiled. "Just a lucky guess."

"Well, you're right. He thought it was a scam. He sent a fake ruby, hoping it would fool them. It didn't, of course—they were criminals, not idiots. The next morning, the butler found the fiancé's body dumped on the front porch. They'd stuffed the phoney ruby into his..." Her cheeks seemed to flush in the moonlight. "Well, you know."

"No," he said politely. "His what?"

She pursed her lips again, her hand fluttering helplessly before her. "His..."

"His briefcase?" She shook her head, so he tried again. "His pocket?" More vigorous shaking. "His nose?"

"His underwear," she finally managed stiffly, avoiding his gaze. "It was some kind of insult, I guess. Symbolic, you know. A little vulgar, maybe, but then they were criminals after all, so that's not surprising." She waved her hand impatiently. "But enough about all that. What he had in his underwear isn't the important part."

Miraculously he didn't even grin. "It isn't?"

"Of course not." Melanie tapped her thumb emphatically against his palm. "Pay attention. The *important* part is that poor Matilda was brokenhearted. She'd lost the only man who would ever love her. Ever. After all, the wart was on her *nose*, poor thing. They say it was *gigantic*!" She pointed to the tip of her nose with her index finger. "Right here. So you see the problem." She lowered her voice. "Kissing, you know. Impossible, just impossible."

She looked sternly at him, and he nodded agreeably, which seemed to satisfy her.

"So there you have it," she concluded mournfully. "Matilda lost her only chance at happiness, at least the good kind, the *kissing* kind, all because her uncle was such a paranoid, stingy old devil."

"Her uncle? I thought you said the old miser was her father."

Melanie frowned. "Of course it was her father. Why on earth would you think it was her uncle?" She coughed softly, grimacing. "Honestly, Clay, I think I ought to know this story better than you do."

He didn't contradict her—what was the point? And besides, he enjoyed hearing her talk.

"It was the same with me," she continued, obviously on a roll now. "Joshua was always afraid that Bill, that's the boy

I eloped with, was after the Browning fortune, too. Only for an hour, though.'' She frowned as if she realized she hadn't made sense. ''I mean I only married him for an hour. At least, that's how it turned out—I expected to be married a hundred times longer than that.'' Another frown. ''Well, you know what I mean.''

''Yes,'' he said. ''Joshua told me that he followed you to Vegas and managed to get the marriage annulled.''

She nodded. ''What a performance! It was as good as any magic act. He marched right up to Bill, whispered the word 'disinherited' in his ear, and my brand-new husband darn near broke his leg rushing to sign the annulment papers.'' She snorted softly. ''So you see? My story is just like Matilda's. Except, of course, that in my story the boyfriend really *was* just after the money.'' She frowned again, concentration digging little shadowy furrows between her brows. ''I guess that's a pretty big difference, isn't it?''

He decided not to answer that. ''Was your heart broken, too? Like Matilda's?''

More furrowing. She sighed heavily, as if she had to think so hard about the question that it hurt. ''I don't know,'' she said slowly. ''My pride was pretty bruised up. But you know...'' She lowered her voice as if spies were lurking all around the tree house. ''I've never told anyone this before, but when we were saying our vows in that cheesy chapel in Vegas, Bill had a little bit of ketchup in his beard. We'd stopped for fast food on the way, you see, and that red blob of ketchup was just hanging there, and I remember looking at it and trying not to laugh. And then I tried to think of letting him take me to bed....''

Shuddering, she drew her legs up to her chest and propped her chin on her knees, staring down at her bare toes. ''So I guess I didn't *really* love him, you know? I mean, when you're married for a whole lifetime, eventually you're going to have to cope with a little ketchup.'' She screwed up her face at the thought. ''Or worse.''

''Yeah.'' He nodded. ''Like coleslaw. Coleslaw would be worse.''

She bestowed a beaming smile on him for understanding so well. "Anyhow, that's the Browning tradition. The old misers can't quite stomach their warty daughters, so they can't believe that anyone else could love them, either."

Her voice was full of light cynicism, but her fingers told Clay a different story. Though she didn't seem to realize it, throughout her recital she had clutched his hand tightly, the way a child might clutch a favorite blanket.

He had to struggle to keep his hand passive beneath that warm, trusting touch. Every human instinct ordered him to take her in his arms, to assure her that Joshua had been blind, that her fortune was the least of her many charms.

But he couldn't do any such thing.

"Face me, Melanie," he said quietly. "Let me look at you."

She turned her head obediently, and for a long moment he scanned her lovely features. He studied everything, from the soft widow's peak of dark hair that shaped her face into a perfect heart, all the way down to the perky, pointed chin that was really too fragile to contain such stubborn defiance.

"Good news," he said as lightly as he could. "No warts."

She instinctively brought her fingers to her nose as if afraid she might suddenly have sprouted a disfiguring growth. Then she smiled behind her fingers, obviously realizing how silly that was.

"No, no warts." She let her hand fall away. "Think there's hope for me, then?"

He nodded. "I predict that you'll know a great deal of happiness in your life."

She gazed at him with laughing eyes. "The good kind? The kissing kind?"

He took a deep breath, cursing the involuntary warmth that rushed to his loins when she looked at him like that. "All kinds," he said firmly, trying to convince himself that he didn't have a body, at least not from the waist down.

"But the kissing kind," she said thoughtfully, staring at his mouth, "is really the best kind." She ran the tip of her tongue

NO COST! NO OBLIGATION TO BUY!
NO PURCHASE NECESSARY!

PLAY "LUCKY 7"
AND GET AS MANY AS 5 FREE GIFTS...

HOW TO PLAY:

1 With a coin, carefully scratch away the silver panel opposite. Then check the claim chart to see what we have for you – FREE BOOKS & GIFTS – ALL YOURS! ALL FREE!

2 Send back this card and you'll receive specially selected Mills & Boon novels from the Presents™ series. These books are yours to keep absolutely FREE.

3 There's no catch. You're under no obligation to buy anything. We charge nothing for your first shipment. And you don't have to make any minimum number of purchases – not even one!

4 The fact is thousands of readers enjoy receiving books by mail from the Reader Service™. They like the convenience of home delivery and they like getting the best new romance novels at least a month before they are available in the shops. And of course postage and packing is completely FREE!

5 We hope that after receiving your free books you'll want to remain a subscriber. But the choice is yours – to continue or cancel, any time at all! So why not take up our invitation, with no risk of any kind. You'll be glad you did!

We all love mysteries... so as well as your free books, there may also be an intriguing gift waiting for you! Simply scratch away the silver panel and check the claim chart to see what you can receive.

Play

"Lucky 7"

P8KI

Just scratch away the silver panel with a coin. Then check below to see how many FREE GIFTS will be yours.

YES! I have scratched away the silver panel. Please send me all the gifts for which I qualify. I understand that I am under no obligation to purchase any books, as explained on the opposite page. I am over 18 years of age.

MRS/MS/MISS/MR _____ INITIALS _____

BLOCK CAPITALS PLEASE

SURNAME _____

ADDRESS _____

_____

POSTCODE _____

7 7 7	**WORTH 4 FREE BOOKS** PLUS AN INTRIGUING MYSTERY GIFT
🔔🔔🔔	**WORTH 4 FREE BOOKS**
⬭⬭⬭	**WORTH 3 FREE BOOKS**
🍒🍒 BAR	**WORTH 2 FREE BOOKS**

slowly, unconsciously, over her lower lip. "Don't you think so?"

Thank God he wasn't standing up. His knees would have buckled under the flood of heat that shot down his thighs. His heartbeat tripped on itself.

"It can be," he said carefully.

"It *was*, for us," she said. "Wasn't it? When you kissed me in the pool, I mean. That was the best kind."

"Yes." He couldn't lie, though he knew he should. "Yes, it was."

Sighing, she brought his hand to her face, resting his palm against her cheek. "It wasn't enough," she said. "You knew that. You knew I wanted you to kiss me again."

Dear God, it was beyond what anyone could bear. The hitch in his breathing had become a pain. This mustn't happen. He tried to breathe through the overwhelming desire. She was drunk. He mustn't take advantage....

"Well, it's not too late, is it?" She smiled again, but beneath the teasing he heard a raw note of real need. Just under her jaw, a pulse beat heavily against the heel of his hand. "You could kiss me now."

If only he could... He remembered her kiss. It had tasted of chlorine, misty innocence and a small, blinding zap of secret electricity.

Civilization was so damned unfair, he thought, suddenly angry. Somewhere outside these cedar walls, the wind laid soft fingers on the leaves, making them shift and whisper. Somewhere out there, the moonlight spilled itself without shame into the deepest shadows of the night.

But in here there was no freedom. There was only a stabbing desire that must never be acknowledged, an aching need that must never be met.

"Melanie," he said softly, through a tightened throat that nearly refused to form the syllables. "Melanie, you've had too much to drink."

"Yes," she said, her lips curving, catching moonlight in their dimpled edges. "Isn't it wonderful?"

He smiled in spite of his body's agony. He couldn't remember when innocence had ever been so seductive, so utterly erotic. But it was still innocence. And he was still a gentleman even though he didn't feel like one, didn't want to be one, didn't even remember why the world thought it was such a goddamn noble thing to be.

"It's time to go inside now," he said gently. Maybe that was what it meant. To be *gentle*, to take this innocence in his hands like a lost bird and carry it back to safety. "It's time for you to go to bed."

He tucked her chin between his thumb and forefinger and lowered it, bringing her gaze level with his. She looked at him for several long seconds, until slowly, millimeter by cruel millimeter, her dreamy smile faded, transforming itself into a confused frown.

"To bed..." Her voice trembled, held aloft on the knifepoint of disappointment. "Do you mean...alone?"

It nearly killed him. But somehow, from that little bag of civilized tricks all gentlemen possessed, he pulled forth the courage. "Yes," he said. "Alone."

CHAPTER SEVEN

SEVERAL days later, Clay let himself in through the front entry of Cartouche Court. Amazingly it was only seven o'clock—he was home for dinner for the first time all week.

He dropped his briefcase on the floor with a sigh. Sunset streamed through the door behind him, tinting the tiles the color of orange sherbet. It was nice to be back before midnight, before the foyer turned into a silvery black, deadly silent cavern.

It was hardly silent today. As he leafed through the mail, squealing laughter rippled down the staircase from one of the second-floor bedrooms. He tilted his head, listening. Melanie and Nick, perhaps?

But it sounded like several people, more like a party, actually. Suddenly, happy voices broke into a giggling chorus of "A Hundred Bottles of Beer on the Wall." Oh, yes. Definitely a party.

He sighed again, staring at the library door. Cataloguing maps had never held less appeal, but he had neglected the job all week, and it was time to buckle down. He loosened his tie, thumbed free his top button and started across the foyer. But before he had made it halfway to the library, a body came barreling down the stairs, taking the steps two and three at a time.

The flying figure skidded to a halt a few feet from Clay. It was Nick—but not the sulking, grungy sad sack he was accustomed to seeing. This Nick was neat, combed and smiling. His jean shorts were baggy, but they almost fit, and, amazingly, his shirt was not black. And it actually had buttons.

In fact, the only real strange detail was the bright red poncho attached to the back of his shirt with two clothespins. As he'd shot down the stairs, the nylon had billowed out behind him like Superman's cape.

Nick froze in place, a sheepish grin plastered across his rapidly reddening face.

Clay smiled. "Hello," he said politely. "Looking for a telephone booth?"

Chuckling, Nick twisted his arms behind his back, trying to unhook the poncho. "Hi," he managed breathlessly. He appeared to be attempting to tie himself into a square knot. "God—sorry about this. We've just been packing my suitcases, and I...we...I guess everyone started to get a little silly."

Afraid the poor fellow might dislocate a shoulder, Clay reached over and twitched the clothespins loose. The poncho slithered to the floor. Clay held out the pins and, when Nick extended a hand, dropped them wordlessly into his open palm.

"Thanks. It's just that, well, you know, it's my last day. So we were laughing and playing games and..." Nick blew air through his lips like a horse, obviously disgusted with his own stammering. "Just dumb stuff."

"It's your last day?" Clay raised one brow. "I didn't even know you were sick."

Nick laughed. "No, jeez...I'm leaving for camp tomorrow, that's all." He frowned suddenly. "Didn't you...I mean, didn't Melanie tell you?"

Clay somehow kept his face expressionless. "No, she didn't. But I haven't been around much this past week."

That part was certainly true. After their encounter in the tree house he hadn't dared to come home while she was still awake. Resisting her that night had drained his willpower down to the last volt, and it was going to need some recharging before he asked it to handle any more temptation.

But what was this about summer camp? Had the whole plan sprouted up in these past few days? On the face of it, the idea looked terrible. He now knew Melanie's financial situation intimately, and he was well aware she didn't have that kind of cash. And he couldn't quite picture Nick signing up to work for his room and board.

So where the hell had the money come from? Melanie knew that any foolish extravagance right now would be disastrous.

Didn't she? Surely, he thought, *surely* she wouldn't have made such a colossal blunder....

"I'll go see what I can do to help," Clay said, then began ascending the stairs as rapidly as Nick had just flown down them. *Damn it, Melanie*, he thought angrily as he reached the landing, *how could you have been so stupid?*

Nick's room was utter chaos. Every surface was covered with camp paraphernalia—fishing tackle, bug spray, swimming goggles, canteens, backpacks, hiking boots. The bed was invisible beneath stacks of blankets, towels and sheets.

Over by the window, Ted Martin and Mrs. Hilliard were quarreling loudly about the correct way to flick one's wrist while casting a fishing line. Across the room, Nick's new girlfriend—Sunny, Bunny, Honey...something like that—was perched atop the dresser, stitching name tags onto T-shirts and humming along with the radio.

Melanie was kneeling on the floor in the center of everything, her hands on her thighs and a bewildered expression on her face as she contemplated the hopeless discrepancy between the size of Nick's open trunk and the huge pile of clothes next to it.

"They have *got* to be kidding," she grumbled to no one in particular. "Somebody up at Camp Windclimber needs a refresher course in solid geometry."

Clay stopped in the doorway, working to subdue the quick flash of heat that sizzled through him at the sight of her. She looked so lovely in her white shorts and blue-striped sailor shirt. Her hair was loose around her shoulders, sunlight reaching into its chestnut depths and highlighting random strands of red and gold.

God, what was happening to him? He couldn't remember ever reacting like this to a woman before. She innocently knelt there folding clothes, and he began to burn with thoughts of naked nights on satin sheets, of hungry hands on silken skin.

She seemed to sense his presence, but she must have assumed it was her brother returning. She rose and bent deep into the trunk, her bottom in the air. "Bad news, Nick," she said, her voice muffled. "We ran out of room. You're going to wear all twelve sets of underwear on the plane."

"Poor Nick," Clay observed from the doorway. "That sounds uncomfortable."

Melanie popped out of the trunk like a jack-in-the-box, scattering socks. She obviously had thought he was safe at work. When she finally remembered to smile, the effect was tentative, extremely nervous.

Well, that was one question answered. He'd wondered how much she would remember of the tree-house encounter. That smile told him. She remembered plenty.

"Anything I can do to help?" he asked politely.

Grinning a much more enthusiastic welcome, Ted answered from across the room. "Maybe. Think you can make Mel understand that fifteen-year-old boys don't mind wearing the same underwear twice? She's packing this kid for a year at the North Pole, not a month in North Carolina."

Scowling indignantly, Melanie held up a long, printed list. "It's not *me*," she said defensively. "It's all right here. It says *twelve* sets of underclothes, *ten* long-sleeved shirts, *five* blue jean shorts—"

"And a partridge in a pear tree," Ted finished in a teasing singsong.

Melanie wrinkled her nose toward Ted and rustled the list at him irritably.

"I need to talk to Melanie anyway," Clay said. "If you'll let me borrow her for a minute, I'll be sure to address the underwear issue while I'm at it."

Blanching almost comically, Melanie stared at him. But Ted chuckled. "Borrow her as long as you want," he said. "She's driving us all crazy with that list."

Clay met Melanie's gaze, wishing that she didn't look so horrified. A little embarrassment about the other night couldn't account for this level of terror. She must be feeling guilty as sin about something, and he could easily guess what. She didn't want to have to explain to him how a woman who had only $87.50 in her checking account last Monday could suddenly come up with enough money to finance a fun-filled month at Camp Windclimber.

He was actually relieved to see her hair hadn't been shorn from her head, sold for size twelve hiking boots and bug spray. But visions of maxed-out credit cards rose before him, complete with double-digit interest rates.

"Melanie?" He kept his invitation cordial.

She rose slowly, extricating herself from the piles of clothes, and followed him out the door. As they crossed the hall, they heard the voices behind them begin to sing. "On the first day of summer camp, my sister gave to me...twelve B.V.D.s..."

She made a small, irritated growl under her breath, but she didn't speak. She walked just a step behind Clay, joining him without protest as he entered the first bedroom on the other side of the hall.

It turned out to be the Gothic room, and it was ironically reminiscent of a torture chamber. Its black iron wall sconces simulated flickering firelight but provided little illumination. Its heavy, ornately carved wooden chairs, stone gargoyles on the mantel and red velvet drapes all looked like something out of an Edgar Allan Poe story.

She swallowed hard but lifted her chin. "Good choice," she said wryly. "An appropriate spot for an inquisition, wouldn't you say?"

"It would be if this *were* an inquisition," he said. "But it isn't."

"What is it, then?"

He set his jaw. Obviously she was *not* feeling cooperative. He knew her well enough now to recognize when she was climbing on her high horse. "It's called a conversation. I just want to know why you didn't tell me you were sending Nick to summer camp."

"I was going to." Avoiding his gaze, she fingered the pierced Gothic tracery on the thronelike back of the nearest chair. "But we decided very suddenly, and you were always at work, and—"

"And you knew I would disapprove?"

She looked up. "Yes, I knew you'd disapprove." Her eyes

were unexpectedly steady. "I knew you'd think I was spoiling him. That's always what you think. But I was going to tell you. I was waiting for the right moment so I could explain all the details."

He laughed, a short, hard sound. "Oh, I think I understand fairly well, even without the details. It's simple. You've done God-knows-what-to-get God-knows-how-much money, so that you can keep right on giving that overindulged kid every damned thing his heart desires."

She tightened her mouth. "You've certainly put the worst possible spin on it."

"Spin it your way, then." He leaned against the wall. "I'm listening."

She glared at him for a moment, then lowered herself wearily into the chair, resting her head against the carved back. "I honestly don't understand why you're so upset. What's so terrible about my sending Nick to summer camp?"

"Maybe nothing." He shrugged. "If it's free."

Her eyes flickered. Not free, then, he thought dryly. What a surprise.

"How much?"

She lifted her chin. "Two thousand dollars."

Two thousand? "Good Lord, Melanie. What the hell were you thinking?"

Her eyes flashed. "I was thinking that this was the first time since Uncle Joshua died that Nick had shown any real enthusiasm for anything. I was thinking that the discipline of summer camp might be good for him. I was thinking that he offered to work to help pay for it, which is also a first."

"Were you thinking about the balance in your checking account, which is a couple of zeros short of being able to finance this little adventure?"

"Yes, damn it, I was!" She looked really angry now, her cheeks flushed. "You always think the worst of me, don't you, Clay? Uncle Joshua must have gotten to you big time. Somehow he convinced you that I'm a birdbrain who balances her checkbook with her fingers, and that Nick's some kind of demon child who's headed straight for the state penitentiary."

"Well, moments like this don't do much to change my mind."

She made fists in her lap. "See what I mean? You don't even know where I got the money or how I intend to pay it back. You don't know anything about this 'moment', and yet you've already entered it as another black mark against my judgment."

"Then tell me," he said tightly. "Tell me how you pulled off this miracle."

"I borrowed two thousand dollars from my bank," she said, obviously struggling to present her case calmly but only partly succeeding. Her blue eyes were still sparking. "Nick has agreed to work off half of it. Ted is going to see that Nick gets enough odd jobs at the school to make that possible. The other half I can pay back myself before the summer is over, by taking a part time job at the school. And, of course, I'll be able to contribute all the money I'm saving in rent by living here."

She subsided as if the effort to defend herself had drained her. She leaned back in the chair, but her eyes watched him, covertly assessing his reaction.

He took a breath, trying to control his frustration. Couldn't she see that the issue was broader than simply *where* she got the money? Even if her fairy godmother had slipped two thousand gold coins under her pillow, Melanie still shouldn't have done this. Her financial situation, though not completely out of control, was precarious. She had no savings account, no emergency cash stashed away, no college fund for Nick. No indication, in short, that she knew tomorrow even existed. Any windfalls should have been banked immediately, not wired off to Camp Windclimber.

He hadn't felt free to guide her—he was supposed to be evaluating her maturity, not creating it like some Svengali. And yet he had hoped against hope that she would deposit the savings she accrued by living free here at Cartouche Court. It would have looked so good on paper. And it would have played so well in court, where they were bound to end up if he gave her the Browning fortune.

Still, he tried to be fair. It was something of a relief to see that she had any plan at all for repayment. And having Nick work to foot part of the bill was an excellent idea. If only he'd really do it.

"You'd be proud of Nick," she said as if reading his mind—or perhaps just reading the skepticism on his features. "He's worked like a fiend all week, mowing lawns and painting things at the school. He's already earned a hundred and fifty dollars. That's a lot, you know, for a fifteen-year-old boy to earn in one week."

He noted the defensive pride in her voice. He could see it made her happy to be able to report that Nick had finally done a some long-overdue work. But then he remembered the neatly combed, smiling Superboy he had encountered in the foyer—maybe she *was* bringing the kid around, at least a little.

Amazing. Rewarding sullen brattiness with a trip to summer camp wouldn't have been *his* preferred method of rehabilitation, but perhaps he didn't really know very much about parenting.

Looking at Melanie now, at her only half-camouflaged eagerness to win his approval, it suddenly occurred to him that she didn't know much about it, either. She had been thrust into guardianship of Nick only a year ago, at a notoriously difficult phase of a teen's development. She was his sister, not his mother—only nine years older than the boy, with no experience at all, no history of authority to fall back on. Perhaps she was doing a better job than he'd given her credit for.

"You know," she said tensely, apparently misinterpreting his long silence, "when we came to Cartouche Court, you said the proximity might help you to get to know us better. But, quite honestly, I don't see you making any effort at all to do that, and I'm not sure that's fair, especially to Nick. He's a pretty nice kid, once you get past the surface."

He gave her a quizzical smile. "I've spent hours studying your financial situation," he said. "That tells me a lot."

"But it doesn't really tell you about *us*," she argued. "It doesn't tell you who we are, what our values are, why we do the things we do."

He wondered whether he should debate this. She had no idea how much he'd learned about her during these past few weeks. Though he had been away a lot, when he was here, he seemed to be intensely aware of every move she made, every sound she uttered. It was as if his receptors were involuntarily—and unalterably—tuned to her frequency.

He knew, for instance, that she curled up in her window seat reading until very late every night. He knew that she sang old ballads in the shower, her sweet voice missing half the notes. He knew that Fudge had adopted her instantly and now unfailingly slept in her room.

He knew that she wasn't accustomed to drinking, that she always parked off center, that she was rotten at darts. He knew she looked adorable in armor and that her foot tapped whenever she heard good dancing music.

He knew that, though her record keeping was abysmal, she'd never missed a single payment on anything. He knew she went barefoot as often as possible, watched too many cop shows on television and cut her own hair.

Hell, he knew more about Melanie than he'd known about his last two lovers.

She stood, waxing indignant as she warmed to her subject. "It seems to me that you've already made up your mind, that you've taken Joshua's word for everything. I mean, with the exception of that one afternoon in the pool, you haven't spent any ti—"

"You do remember what happened when we were in the pool, don't you?" He raised his brows. "If I spend very much time getting to know you *that* well, I'll have to turn this decision over to someone else or risk getting disbarred."

She flushed a deep scarlet, almost the same color as the drapes behind her head. "I didn't mean," she said awkwardly. "I know that was...we both understand that it wasn't, shouldn't ever have..."

She shifted uncomfortably, and he knew she was remembering the night in the tree house, too. She pulled nervously on her ear and didn't quite look at him.

He came closer, close enough to touch her shoulder. "Relax, Melanie," he said. "I do know what you meant. And I promise you I haven't decided anything yet. In fact, you're actually changing my mind about quite a few things." He smiled. "While Nick's away, maybe we'll have some time to talk things over."

She tentatively returned his smile, obviously hearing the apology that was buried in the sentences and accepting it. That was another thing he had learned about her: The only grudge she seemed capable of sustaining was against Joshua.

"You know, I could help you with the maps," she said. "I always wanted to learn more about them, but Joshua didn't like to be disturbed when he was working."

He hesitated, wondering whether his overtaxed willpower could stand many nights sequestered in the library with only Copernicus as chaperon. But the look on her face was too helpful. He found that he couldn't resist it.

Great. Pretty soon he'd be as spineless as she was. Well, at the very least, this should teach him more sympathy for the way she spoiled Nick. Apparently there really were times when "no" was just too damned hard to say.

To Melanie's surprise, the evenings spent helping Clay with the maps quickly settled into a comfortable pattern. As soon as he returned from the office each night, they ate dinner, which had been fixed by Mrs. Hilliard and left in the oven to warm. Then they carried their coffee cups into the library and spent at least half an hour just sipping and chatting, unwinding before they tackled the real work.

At first, Melanie had felt terribly stilted, holding a tight rein on herself for fear she'd talk too much, laugh too loudly, lapse into the kind of silly horseplay she had such a regrettable tendency to enjoy. But Clay seemed to go out of his way to be friendly and set her at ease. And Copernicus was always so ridiculous he made Melanie look tame by comparison.

The parrot broke the ice on the very first night, hanging upside down on his swing by one foot and by commanding them to admire him by calling, "Hey, hey, hey!" Loving the attention, he soon overplayed the game, slipped off and bonked his head on the bottom of the cage.

When Clay and Melanie began to laugh, the parrot let loose a string of clearly furious but often nonsensical insults. Among other things, he called them ''goddamn reproductions'', proving that, although he'd listened to Uncle Joshua, he hadn't always necessarily understood him.

It was hard to be stiff and distant after that. Before long, Melanie found herself chattering away as if she had known Clay forever. Two weeks later, when she realized Nick's summer-camp experience was more than halfway over, she could hardly believe it.

''I've missed him terribly,'' she told Clay as they finished their coffee that night. ''But it's been nice not to have to worry about him every day. I haven't had to say, 'Do your homework, you lazy slug,' for two whole weeks now. Even better, for those two weeks, no one has snarled at me and said, 'Jeez, Mel, get off my back.''' She stretched and sighed. ''Ah, freedom!''

Clay smiled. ''You're working two part-time jobs, plus helping me out with the maps, and you call that freedom?''

She knew it sounded odd. ''I don't mind work. I *like* to work. It's the responsibility for a hormonally challenged teenager that's so exhausting. It's nagging him to do his chores. Wondering whether I've been too tough or too lax. Checking his bed ten times a night to be sure he hasn't sneaked out. That's what's exhausting.''

He looked at her quizzically. ''*Ten* times?''

''Okay, maybe only once or twice,'' she admitted with a grin. ''But still, I haven't had a good night's sleep since I found that bottle of gin squirreled away in the tree house.''

She slanted a look at him through her lashes, wondering what he really thought about that night. During these past two weeks, she and Clay had discussed everything from asparagus to the afterlife, but they hadn't once mentioned how he'd caught her trying to pour herself into a bottle of gin.

''Ah, yes, Nick's secret stash of liquor.'' He chuckled as he opened a portfolio of maps. "I must say you found a creative way to dispose of that little problem."

She grimaced. "It may have been creative," she said, "but it was painful. When I woke up the next morning, I thought I was going to die."

"Oh, hangovers never kill you. That would be too easy."

His voice was warm with amused understanding, and watching his lazy smile, she felt a sudden geyser of gratitude. He could easily have adopted a censorious tone, expressing disapproval of her excesses. Instead he was acting as if it had been no big deal, as if he carried drunken, love-starved women down out of trees every Friday night.

"It wasn't just the hangover," she said, her voice strangely shaky. "Humiliation can be pretty lethal, too, you know."

He glanced up from the map he'd been studying, his hands still as they gripped the edges of the paper. "Humiliation?" He tilted his head. "I don't think anything you did calls for quite as strong a word as that."

She looked at him. The desk lamp gilded one side of his face, accentuating the high cheekbone and the strong, beautiful bow of his lips. It was all too easy to remember why she had wanted him to kiss her. His face was the most intriguing blend of knock-you-over virility and intelligent, self-effacing humor.

However, she couldn't keep staring at him. Clearing her throat, she picked up her notebook and opened it to a blank page, ready to copy down his dictation. Her pen was poised, but she couldn't help wondering whether she would be able to keep her mind focused on dates, folio numbers, printing techniques and watermarks.

She couldn't. She laid her pen on the table behind her, next to one of Uncle Joshua's antique handcuffs, then cleared her throat again. Clay looked up from his map.

"I want to apologize for the way I acted that night," she said, trying to sound calm. It had to be discussed sooner or later. Sooner was better. Braver. More mature. And wasn't that what Joshua had wanted? "I'm fairly fuzzy on some of it, but I'm pretty sure that I was..." She met his gaze miserably.

"Well, that I more or less threw myself at you. There's no excuse for it—all I can say is that I'm not used to liquor."

"So I assumed," he said lightly. "Gin actually shouldn't throw off your aim until a few inches into the second bottle."

She could have kissed him for making this so easy for her. But that, she reminded herself ruefully, was how she'd gotten into this mess in the first place. Contenting herself with a grateful smile, she let out a deep breath. "Anyway, I'm very sorry. I hope we can forget it ever happened and move on."

He lifted one corner of his mouth. "I had hoped so, too," he said. "But I have to admit that so far I'm not having much success."

She flushed. "Oh, dear," she said, covering her embarrassment with a light laugh. "That bad?"

He chuckled softly. "No," he murmured. "That *good*."

She felt her flush deepening, a thick warmth that seemed to seep through her veins like a heavy syrup. He was looking at her mouth, and she tucked her lower lip between her teeth as if to hide it. She tried to think of a cute comeback, one that would be in keeping with their newfound, uncomplicated friendship, but her mind was as blank as the sheet of paper she held on her lap.

That two-week-old "friendship" seemed to have vanished again, like a firefly into the night. They were back to uneasy, spine-tingling attraction.

"Good," she ventured hesitantly, "but inappropriate."

He was still looking at her mouth. "Wildly."

"And ill-advised."

"Completely."

"And never to be repeated."

"Only in my dreams," he said in a low voice. He hesitated. "You do understand that, don't you, Melanie?"

She nodded. Of course she did. Their relationship was professional, and he couldn't stray across the strict ethical lines that his job had drawn between them. She understood only too clearly. His loyalty belonged, in the end, to Joshua.

But her fingers began to throb painfully, and she realized she was holding her steno pad so tightly she'd bent it.

Perhaps Joshua had been right. Perhaps she *was* hopelessly immature. She ought to be thankful that Clay was willing to overlook her indiscretions. She ought to be satisfied with the happy knowledge that, at least in some small degree, the desire she felt for him had been reciprocated. But she was like a child who wasn't satisfied to be given half a candy bar. She wanted more. She wanted everything.

All she could think was how wonderful it would be if he would stand up right now, walk across this golden-shadowed room and take her in his arms. All she could think was that she wanted him, wanted him so intensely that her heart was lodged in her throat, as large and hard and rough as the Romeo Ruby.

And she could never have him.

As if they were pieces on a chessboard, Joshua had diabolically positioned them so that they were tantalizingly close but unable to move one inch closer without disaster.

Congratulations, Joshua, she thought bitterly. *You win again.*

CHAPTER EIGHT

"OKAY, bombs away!"

Positioning herself directly beside the two-story library ladder, Melanie cupped her hands in front of her, creating a target for Clay to hit when he dropped his next and, she hoped, final research book.

His aim was impeccable. The tome came whistling down, gathering speed over the twelve vertical feet and landing in her arms with a heavy thud. She sneezed as dust puffed up in a small gray cloud.

Twitching her itching nose, she plopped the thick book on top of the other two dozen he'd already selected from the endless rows of mahogany shelves. "All right, that's enough," she said firmly, waving the dust away. "If you can't find what you need in one of these, you're not looking hard enough."

"One more," he said absently, rubbing a spine to study the title. "And stop complaining. You just have to catch the darn things. I'm going to have to read them."

Melanie scowled at the books, which were, in her estimation, the most boring-looking volumes she'd ever seen. They made even Milton look like fun, she thought.

"No, doggone it. No more," she said rebelliously. As Clay began to slide the rolling ladder toward another panel, she impulsively grabbed one of the bottom rungs and held on. "Clay, it's midnight. You've got to be ready for a break. A snack, maybe? I could make popcorn."

"As soon as I find this last book," he said, almost to himself. "It might be over there, with the London maps." He tried to shove the ladder to the right. "Hey. Let go."

Instead she clenched her fingers tighter, holding the ladder in place. "C'mon," she begged. "You've got to be hungry. Milk and cookies? Scotch and soda? Chopped liver and jelly beans?"

"Ugh." He finally glanced down at her over his shoulder. "Together?"

"Not necessarily." Grinning, she jostled the ladder lightly. "I could eat in the kitchen if you'd like."

He sighed, but his lips tucked in at the corners as if he barred a smile with effort. "Melanie Browning, did you know that you're a pain in the ass?"

Smiling up at him, she slid the ladder six inches in the wrong direction. "Yep."

"And incredibly stubborn?"

She raised one brow in a pretty good imitation of his own sardonic expression. "Actually," she sniffed, "I prefer 'headstrong'."

"Is that so?" He narrowed his eyes. "Well, did you know that if you don't let go of this ladder, I'll come down and tie a knot in your headstrong little ponytail?"

She jiggled the ladder back and forth, unimpressed. "Copernicus will protect me," she said loftily. But a quick glance over toward the perch wasn't reassuring. The bird was babbling to himself in his little mirror, obviously fascinated by his own reflection. She wrinkled her nose. "Don't let appearances fool you. Copernicus is a highly trained attack parrot."

"Right. And I'm one of the Flying Mandini Brothers." Clay swiveled, pointing one long forefinger down at her, shaking it with a slow, half-teasing intensity. "This is your last warning, Ms. Browning. Let go of this ladder or suffer the consequences."

"Well, fine!" She released the rung with an offended flourish. "Suit yourself. Starve if you want to. I, however, am going to get some popcorn." She backed away, watching his face for reaction. He *had* to be hungry. "Yep, that's where I'll be, in the kitchen, popping some hot...delicious...buttery—"

She stopped abruptly, choking out a meaningless, half-strangled syllable as her calves bumped into the forgotten tower of books. And then, with only that half second's warning, she was suddenly tumbling forward, staggering helplessly, falling in slow motion like some kind of circus clown.

She flung out her hand, instinctively trying to catch herself, but it was impossible. Dust billowed as the stack of books crashed around her ankles, tangling her feet into helpless knots and pitching her straight into the ladder.

"Clay!" But she knew even as she called out that her warning was too late. The ladder jerked under her weight, shooting across its track several feet before it crashed into the corner and stopped there, nearly quivering from the force.

She heard a cruel whack as Clay slammed into the molding. His body lurched, and Melanie's breath froze. He had been caught off guard. He was going to fall....

"Clay!" Melanie scrambled to her feet, clambering across the fallen books, rushing toward him as if somehow she could catch him, as if she could break that terrible, twelve-foot drop. "Oh, God, Clay..."

But miraculously he didn't fall. She clasped her hands to her breast, looking up. God only knew how he had done it, but he was still safely on the ladder, his arms straining to hold his body in place. He found his footing with one deft motion and then, amazingly, he was descending, calling her name in an anxious, guttural voice.

She ran to him, crashing into his arms. "Oh, God," she murmured as her hands wrapped around his back. 'Oh, Clay, I'm so sorry."

He touched her hair softly. "It's okay, Melanie. I'm fine." He bent his head over her. "What about you? Are you okay?"

She nodded. "Yes," she murmured into the downy blue cotton of his shirt. "Just shaken a little." She swallowed hard and looked up at him. "I thought you were going to fall. If you had fallen from way up there, you could have...you might have..."

He chuckled quietly. "Didn't I warn you it wasn't that easy to kill me?" He touched her chin. "I used to do that act all the time with the Flying Mandini Brothers."

Though she smiled, she held on to him, as if she could reassure herself of his safety only by feeling his warmth under her palms. Though he didn't resist, she noticed that he didn't return the embrace, holding his arms and hands stiffly.

"Button your face, pinhead," Copernicus demanded grumpily from his perch, obviously irritated by the commotion but not at all concerned about the welfare of his human companions. "You're giving me a goddamn headache."

Clay's chest moved in silent laughter. "I love you, too, birdbrain," he said in a mocking murmur. "Now go back to what you were doing."

His only answers were a noisy spate of irate wing ruffling and a few unintelligible mutterings that might have been German.

Melanie smiled into Clay's shirt, tightening her fingers against his shoulders. The pressure made him flinch suddenly, and he sucked in his breath with a small, hissing sound.

She drew back. "You are hurt!"

He shook his head. "Just a couple of annoyed tendons registering a formal complaint," he said with studied nonchalance. "Though I guess I probably ought to do something about this arm before I drip all over Joshua's extremely expensive carpet."

Her gaze flew down—and she bit her lip, suppressing a cry of horrified surprise. Blood was seeping from a gouge about two inches long on the inside of his forearm. "My God," she breathed. "What happened?"

He shrugged stiffly, and she noticed his features tightened with pain as he moved even that little bit. No wonder he hadn't returned her embrace. His tendons were more than annoyed. They were probably sprained, or even torn. And his arm...

"There must be an exposed nail or screw head along the ladder," he said, tilting his wrist to contain the blood. "When I caught myself, I guess I tore my arm on it."

She cupped her hands under his elbow, as if somehow just by cradling it she could make it better. Taking a deep breath, she tried to remember the name of Joshua's doctor, who used to live nearby. She couldn't see much beneath the blood, but she suspected the gash would require stitches.

"Hey, there." Tugging on a lock of her hair, Clay smiled down at her reassuringly. "It's not so bad. Just think of it as a drastic way of making me take a break. Now we can finally have that midnight snack."

She made a small tssking sound behind her teeth. Here he was, bleeding half to death, and he was reassuring *her*?

"We'll see what the doctor says," she returned briskly, leading him across the room toward the kitchen, her hands still cupped under his arm. "I have a feeling you're not going to be snacking on anything but aspirin and antibiotics."

His brows tugged together. "I don't need a doctor."

"Yes, you do."

"Melanie." His voice was stern. "It's just a scratch. Don't be ridiculous."

Just a scratch? The blood was running down his forearm like the tributaries of the reddest river on any of Uncle Joshua's maps. Honestly, she thought, dabbing at the blood with a tissue, sometimes men were just too macho to live.

"Listen, Clay Logan, I won't be responsible for your bleeding to death. You're going to let a doctor at this if I have to grab one of those medieval handcuffs over there, chain you to the kitchen table and force the man to sew it up at swordpoint."

His frown deepened, and she thought for a moment she was in for a fight. Then a twinkle began to dawn slowly in the depths of his brown eyes. "You'd do it, too, wouldn't you?" His voice was muffled, as if he was hiding a smile.

"You bet I would," she said, struggling to keep her own austere expression intact. "I'm always happiest, you know, when I'm wielding a weapon."

Two hours later, when they were down to the hard yellow kernels in the bottom of the popcorn bowl, Melanie finally saw Clay's muscles relax. His mouth relinquished its thin edge of pain. His eyes softened as if they had lost their focus. With a deep sigh, he put his feet up on the sofa and let his head fall against the thickly padded arm.

"I should have had coffee," he said, rubbing his fingers across the bridge of his nose. "I've got a lot more work to do tonight. Ridiculous to be feeling so damn sleepy."

It was about time, she thought, sneaking a peek at her watch. It had been an hour since she'd crushed up two of the high-powered pain pills the doctor had left and slipped them into Clay's drink. She'd begun to think she should have used three.

But she hadn't dared. The doctor had said just one pill would be enough to kill most of Clay's pain from his sprained shoulder and stitched forearm. Surely, she'd thought, two would be enough to eliminate *all* of it and make him take a good, long, restorative nap without doing any harm. Three…well, three would have been excessive, maybe even dangerous. She'd come close enough to killing him already tonight.

"Are you sleepy, too, Melanie?" He smiled fuzzily and patted the sofa cushion next to him. "There's room for both of us here." He poked Fudge with one sock-clad toe. "Or there will be if I can make this lazy cat disappear."

Melanie caught her breath. He didn't mean it, of course. In his normal frame of mind, he would be horrified to realize he had even uttered such words. Besides, he'd probably be asleep in a very few minutes. His lids were heavy, lowering over his eyes in a completely unintentional sensuality. The shivering thrill intensified, and Melanie had to clamp her teeth together to control it.

He wasn't himself, didn't know what he was saying. *Remember that, you dreamer.*

She stroked Fudge's back, enjoying the soft rumble of his purring under her fingers. The cat obviously had no intention of going anywhere. Clay continued to prod with his toe, but Fudge didn't even open his eyes, much less move a muscle.

"I think Fudge wants you all to himself," she observed wryly. "Or perhaps he thinks he's protecting your virtue."

"Great. Now I'm being chaperoned by a cat." Clay's eyes drifted shut, but he wasn't quite asleep. His lips were curved in an adorable half smile, and he nuzzled one toe behind Fudge's ear, which set off a storm of purring. "Relax, buddy. I'm too tired to pose a threat to anybody's virtue tonight, even my own."

From her cross-legged position on the floor, Melanie watched Clay for a few moments, enjoying her chance to stare without being caught. He was all man, she mused. Even drugged into quiescence, his body emanated virility.

And yet there was warmth, too, in the breadth of his mouth, and humor in the easy curve of his lips. And a marvelous male beauty lurked in the most subtle details: his sable lashes, silken crescents that reached nearly to his cheekbones; the graceful arch of his eyebrows; the perfectly shaped ear that nestled in the waves of his hair.

Suddenly she wanted, with a desire so intense it tightened her throat, to touch his ear, to feather away the soft hair that curled into its seashell whorls.

"Tell me something."

His eyes were half-open again. She flushed. She'd been caught staring after all.

"Anything in particular?" she queried lightly.

One side of his mouth lifted. "Two things, actually." He shifted to his side, favoring the hurt shoulder. He rubbed his palm across the hint of stubble that darkened his jaw. "I was wondering...how do you feel about men in beards these days?"

She smiled. "That depends," she said. "With or without ketchup?"

He grunted. "Either way."

She tried to remember Bill's face, but it seemed so long ago. She could hardly picture him at all.

"Nothing," she said, half-surprised to discover it was really true. No pain, no longing, no lingering cracks from a broken heart. Even the anger and humiliation over that episode seemed to have faded away. "I feel nothing."

He shut his eyes. "Good," he whispered.

She could tell he was drifting off. She ought to let him sleep, but she couldn't resist trying to coax a few more of those unguarded sentences. She'd never hear these things from him once the effects of the drugs wore off.

"Clay," she said softly, touching his shoulder, "what was the second thing you wanted me to tell you?"

His eyes fluttered briefly before shutting again, and she knew from their unfocused gaze that he hardly saw her. Those pain pills must have been as powerful as dynamite—they had blown his concentration, and his inhibitions, to bits.

"The second thing..." He frowned, then smiled as if he'd found the memory, and it delighted him. But he still didn't open his eyes. The conversation might have been taking place in his head. "Tell me," he said. "Those pictures you were throwing darts at in the tree house the other night—was one of them of me?"

She laughed out loud. Of all the questions she might have expected...

"Yes," she admitted. "Yes, it was."

He sighed, burrowing his good shoulder deeper into the recesses of the cushions. His voice had dropped low. "How was your aim? Did you miss me?"

She stood and began to unfold the silk comforter. "Nope," she said, arranging the covers over his body. "Sorry. I hit you dead on, Mr. Logan. Right in the heart."

He chuckled slowly. "Yes," he murmured, his voice slurring as he sank into sleep. "I was afraid of that."

Somewhere in the middle of the night, he woke to the white-roses scent of her, to the tiny, fiery thrill of her fingertips stroking his ear.

He shifted where he lay, confused, groggy and fiercely aroused all at once. He wondered briefly where he was but somehow couldn't open his eyes to check. He was shivering, and yet his veins were hot, as if he was feverish, as if he was ill.

He'd been asleep...and yet he was dressed. He wondered why. His clothes felt too tight. They scraped against his skin. He shifted again, trying to ease the burning tightness between his legs. He must have been dreaming of her, of touching her. *Melanie.*

Time slipped, like a loose chain around the gears of a cosmic clock. When he found himself again, he was groaning, or perhaps the sound was only in his mind. Her slim fingertip was skimming the rim of his outer ear, sliding into the crevices, tracing the folds with a torturous eroticism.

He sucked in his breath hard and flexed his hips, lifting them, seeking relief. His blood beat rhythmically, relentlessly, the ache between his legs so intense he wondered why he wasn't screaming.

He tired to rise, but his body wouldn't obey. The slightest movement shot pain through his shoulder. *What the hell...?* He felt so damn strange. Dizzy, out of control, and yet so sexually charged... What was happening? Was any of this real?

"Melanie," he said again, but this time he said it aloud, his voice floating out, husky and hollow, into the empty air.

Her fingers froze, then pulled sharply away. "Clay," she said in a startled whisper, "I thought you were asleep."

Relief, like a rush of starlight. She was real, then. He opened his eyes, and there she was, kneeling beside him on the sofa, her dark hair loose around her shoulders, her gown and robe bathed in moonbeams from the open dome above them. She leaned forward, white roses swimming toward him on the cool air. He groaned again as his body responded with a flare of heat.

"What is it, Clay?" Her voice was tender, worried. Her fingers cupped his cheek. "Are you in pain?"

"Yes," he said, breathing deeply, thankful that she understood. "Yes."

"Where?" She bent over him, her breasts brushing his chest. "Is it your arm?"

"It's everything." His throat felt hoarse. "I can't breathe. I woke up with your perfume in my lungs."

"My perf—" She straightened abruptly. "Oh, Clay. Clay, no. I didn't mean to—"

"I woke up with your fingers on my skin." He moved his legs, fighting the swelling pain. His head was spinning. Didn't she understand what she had done to him? Couldn't she see? He wanted to take her hand away from his face, wanted to pull it down to where the heat was consuming him. "I woke up wanting you."

She stirred, murmuring a sound of soft distress. "This was

a mistake,'' she said, closing her robe around her throat. ''I'll go—''

''No!''

In desperation, he reached out roughly, his hand encountering cool, liquid fabric and then her warmth beneath. Her eyes were wide with something wild and frightened, but he held on. The room was whirling, and she was the only thing he was sure of.

''Please,'' he rasped. ''Stay.''

She hesitated. Ruthless in his need, driven by the fear that she would leave him, he took advantage of that unguarded moment. He gathered soft layers of silk into his hands. He pulled them apart, lifting lace, separating buttons, seeking her body. Surely she wouldn't stop him. Couldn't she tell he was on fire?

''Clay,'' she whispered in a desperate undertone, her hands brushing his. ''Oh, Clay, you don't want to do this, you can't. Oh, please, remember, you said we mustn't...''

He had said that? Never. How could he have said such a thing? This was destined. Hadn't they known all along that someday it would happen? Desire had been their invisible companion for weeks, driving them both half-insane.

She needed him, too—her words were nonsense. So he ignored her murmured fears, listening instead to the heat of her body, the hum of desire that matched his own. One more button, a low gasp, a slithering collapse of silk—and finally she was his.

He made a dark sound in his throat. Naked, she was almost unbelievably beautiful. As if stunned, she held herself motionless, one hand raised to her throat. From the dome overhead, the moonlight washed her skin in opalescent cream and kissed the graceful curve of her breasts with a milky glow.

''Melanie.'' With a groan, he shifted, wondering why he still felt that lightning bolt in his shoulder when he tried to sit up. But it didn't matter—there were other ways to make love. A hundred ways. And suddenly he wanted them all. He closed his eyes against the blinding rush of pure sexual hunger.

Would his oddly weakened body be strong enough? Would the night be long enough?

Though his lids were heavy, he forced his eyes open again. She was watching him, her lips parted, moonlight creamy blue against her cheeks. Slowly, gently, he touched her with careful absorption, as if he feared he would startle her into vanishing. He still half believed she was merely a mirage.

He dragged his finger along the outer edge of her thigh, tracing the curve of her hip, dipping into the hollow behind her knee, with a hypnotized concentration. So strange, he thought, to be floating in this hypersensual limbo. He felt painfully ready, yet supernaturally patient, as if he could climax in an instant or hold off the end for hours.

He shook his head slightly, trying to clear it. Could this be a dream? Perhaps he was drunk. God knew he felt drugged. He felt incoherent, awed beyond reason by the tiny goose bumps that rose along the surface of her skin.

Time blinked, and he didn't know whether he had been exploring her a split second or a lifetime. But when he looked again, her head was thrown back, her eyes tightly closed. She was breathing shallowly.

"Please stop," she said, touching his hand as if to push it away, but ending with her fingers tangled in his, feverishly clinging. "You know I'm not strong enough. You know I can't resist you."

"Yes," he whispered. "I know."

"This is all my fault." She hesitated as if struggling to breathe. "If I hadn't touched you, if only I hadn't waken you—"

"Shhhh..." He slipped his palm around her thigh, tired of words. He couldn't find any in the fractured spaces of his brain, and hers were noises—sweet, rushing sounds that were as meaningless as water tumbling over moon-washed pebbles. "Just let it happen, Melanie. Make love to me."

Her struggle was silent, heartbreakingly beautiful. She held her knees stiff, her body rigid, as if she could bind herself together with cords of sheer, vibrating tension. She covered her breasts with her palms. One large tear found its way down her cheek, glimmering in the moonlight like an opal on a fragile silver chain.

Finally her willpower simply seemed to run out. Taking in a shuddering breath, she placed her hands on his chest. "Show me," she whispered. "Show me what to do."

It was so easy. He wrapped one palm around her thigh, guiding her. She was fluid and graceful, featherlight as he lifted her and positioned her legs around him.

"Melanie." He could hardly believe how lovely she was. He trailed his hands down the long, curved arch of her back, down to the tender swell of her buttocks. Every inch of her was pure velvet. His own angel-white, musky-midnight rose.

Her muscles quivered where they touched his torso, and he felt an answering stir in his own body. He still wasn't sure where they were or why she had come to him tonight, but this, this helpless need, he understood. The time for silent awe was over.

He pulled her toward him, higher on his chest. With both hands on her hips, he rocked her, tilting her forward up onto her knees, opening her to his probing lips. Raising his head, he nuzzled the soft triangle of curling down. As he took her sweetness between his lips, she tensed, moaning in the back of her throat.

"Clay..." Her fingers clenched in his hair. But she didn't pull away, even when he reached up, slipping two fingers deep into the heart of her.

He waited, and only when he heard her soft, pleading whimper did he begin to move. Guided by her small female sounds, he kissed and stroked with alternate beats, tasting and plundering in a complicated, timeless syncopation.

Murmuring his name, she leaned forward, arching deeply, panting softly. She began to tremble, tiny shudders breaking against his fingers. *Yes*, he thought, both lulled and inflamed by the instinctive rhythms. *Oh, yes, this was right.*

But suddenly, without warning, with only a small, tight cry, she pulled away.

"Melanie, no." He reached for her, catching the liquid satin on her hair between his fingers. "God. No."

She kept sliding down, her soft skin grazing the tightness between his legs. His legs twitched against the pain. Peppering his skin with small, hot kisses, she fumbled with the buttons of his jeans. He couldn't catch his breath. She was lifting his hips, skimming rough denim over his thighs...

As cold moonlight touched him, he groaned. And then, mercifully, she rose again, settling her body around him. Her warm skin met his burning flesh, and he dug his fingers into the leather of the sofa, choking back wild, primitive noises.

As she sank onto him, the moonlight burst into sudden flame so bright he had to shut his eyes against it. Helpless, he watched from the inside as she enveloped him in fire, like the deepest heart of a ruby, like a glittering red prism of need.

The image sparked a sudden memory, a strange, eleventh-hour clarity. Of course. The ruby. Heart-shaped, priceless, throbbing... Why hadn't he realized this long ago? This was the treasure that all men sought, that *he* sought, that he had been seeking all his life.

He felt her body stretching to accept him. She sank deeper, deeper...until he was buried up to the hilt, up to the heart. And there was no escape.

Oh, God...

She began to move, and he thought perhaps he would die. Rising, sinking, lifting and falling. Surrounding him. Driving him mad, forcing harsh groans from his throat.

Melanie...

She rode him. How long? Seconds, hours, aeons? He was spinning in a whirlpool of sensation that banished real time. It left him no thoughts, no words. He wasn't a person; he was merely blood and fire, bursting pleasure and blinding pain. He felt his head thrashing, trying to hold back. *Now, right now, I cannot wait...*

Sweating, aching, wanting. *Please...*

Had he actually begged aloud? Or, even worse, had he demanded as if he could order her to please him?

She must have heard him. She forgave him. Breath raspy, skin slick, she increased the pressure, sped up the pace. Faster. Harder. Taking him home, setting him free. She sobbed, spasmed, trembled, but she drove on. "I love you," she cried suddenly, the words harsh, seemingly torn from a raw, aching throat.

At the sound of her voice, he groaned, thrusting roughly, insane with relief. Though he knew it was too much for her, he couldn't hold back—his body was no longer his own. She shuddered helplessly, calling out his name like a cry for help. And then the room exploded, shooting fire and rainbows, rubies and moonbeams around them in a shower of unimaginable pleasure.

He lost himself in the flood. A lifetime later, damp and gasping, she collapsed against his chest. He clutched her hard, dragging her with him as he began to sink into a deep, bottomless darkness. He fought the fall. He needed... He needed to tell her... But he kept sinking, and the words wouldn't quite come.

He felt her lips move against his skin. *I love you*, she mouthed silently.

Love, he answered somewhere in his drifting mind. That wasn't exactly what he'd meant to say, but somehow it was all he could manage. *Yes. Love. Yes.*

CHAPTER NINE

MELANIE'S fingers were shaking. The coffeepot slipped in her hand, landing on the marble kitchen countertop with a metallic bang. She darted an anxious glance toward the doorway, though she knew that Cartouche Court was much too big for noise to be a problem. She could have smashed every dish in the house without disturbing anyone sleeping in the library.

Still, the clumsy mistake proved just how nervous she was. When had she begun to feel so weak and cowardly? An hour ago, when she had unwrapped Clay's arms from around her shoulders and risen from the leather sofa, she had been fine.

Well, more or less fine... Though she had foolishly wanted to linger, cradled in Clay's warm, muscular body, at first light she had gone upstairs, where she had showered, dressed and brushed her hair, all in a determined calm.

No whining, she had instructed her reflection. No adolescent wringing of hands. She had scrubbed half the enamel off her teeth as if somehow that would relentlessly eradicate every flicker of self-pity.

And no craven rationalizations about having been swept away, she'd insisted ruthlessly, pointing the toothbrush at the pale face in the mirror. Whatever happened this morning, she was going to be honest with herself, however uncomfortable it might be.

Okay. The truth, then. She knew Clay had not wanted last night to happen. And she could have prevented it. Though his hands had been sweeter than dreams, more urgent than life itself, she could have stopped him. She could simply have said no. Instead she had said yes. Consciously, deliberately. With her whole heart, *yes*. In the end, the decision had been quite simple. She had wanted to make love to Clay Logan because it was exactly that: love.

One-sided love, of course. She hadn't fooled herself about

that. Loaded with potent pills, dazed with sleep and pain, Clay had barely realized what he was doing. Throughout the entire experience, his eyes had remained strangely unfocused. His movements, though expert and seductive, had possessed the blind fluidity of instinct. And he had sunk back into a deep, drugged sleep immediately after....

She, however, had no such excuses. She had known there would be a price to pay, and that the bill would come due with the dawn.

As the trembling began again, she measured out the coffee grounds with unnatural deliberation, trying to stay focused. *One, two, three...* Strong, it should be strong. He'd need plenty of caffeine to shake the effects of the pills. *Four, five...* She dropped the spoon with another clatter. She made fists on the counter and bent over, trying to swallow the fluttering that pulsed at her throat.

One last, desperate idea presented itself. Perhaps, she thought, dusting the spilled coffee grounds into her palm, he wouldn't quite believe that it had really happened. Maybe he'd think it had all been a dream. After all, she'd given him a *lot* of painkiller—

"Call me old-fashioned," a sour voice from behind her said suddenly, "but I've found it works better if you actually plug the pot in."

Melanie looked up, horrified to see Mrs. Hilliard standing in the doorway that led from the housekeeper's wing. "Oh," she said stupidly. She reached for the cord. "Right. Sorry."

"Don't apologize to me," the older woman grumbled. "I don't drink that swill. Eats the lining right out of your stomach." She glared at the refrigerator. "You left the door open," she added, flattening her palm against the offending surface and pressing hard. Melanie watched numbly as Mrs Hilliard turned toward the pantry and began sorting through the alphabetized shelves of canned goods. She cocked her head toward Melanie, still scowling. "Oatmeal?"

"No, thank you," Melanie managed through tight lips. "I'll just have a doughnut."

The older woman grunted, condemning all pastries and

everyone who ate them. She lifted a cantaloupe the size of a bowling ball from the refrigerator and thrust it toward Melanie. "Eat this. That other slop will clog your arteries like gear grease."

Melanie gritted her teeth, but she took the cantaloupe rather than argue the state of her circulatory system before eight o'clock on a Sunday morning. She set the melon on the counter with a subtly defiant thud. What was Mrs. Hilliard doing here anyway? The woman never set foot in the kitchen on a Sunday. Never. Even God rested one day a week, she'd been fond of saying. For years, whenever Melanie had thought of God, she'd pictured him in a white uniform, looking weirdly like Mrs. H.

So why had she picked today to change the habits of a lifetime? Why this particular Sunday, when Melanie would have traded the Romeo Ruby itself for an hour alone with Clay? How could they sort things out with Mrs. Doomsday hanging around?

The housekeeper returned to organizing the pantry, her back eloquently presented to Melanie, who rummaged as quietly as possible for a knife. All she could find was a meat cleaver. It was a clumsy business to quarter the cantaloupe with that huge, flat blade, but frankly, before she'd ask Mrs. Hilliard for help, she'd hack the darn thing open with a pair of nail scissors.

The coffeepot burbled beside her, like a foot soldier jerking to attention now that the general had arrived. Melanie held the cantaloupe over the sink, trying to pry seeds out with the edge of the cleaver. Soon the fruit looked traumatized, a wet, fleshy hash.

"Good morning."

Melanie's heart stood still. It was Clay. Staring into the sink, she kept working the cleaver against the pitiful, lacerated cantaloupe, unable to force herself to turn around.

"Would you look at her?" Mrs. Hilliard didn't bother with pleasantries. She moved right into her favorite pastime—criticizing Melanie. "Would you look at the size of that knife she's using on that poor piece of fruit?"

Melanie's pulse thudded as she waited for Clay to make some indolently sarcastic remark about her affinity for lethal weapons. *Tease me, Clay*, she willed silently. *I know we can't be real lovers, but please...show me that we can still be friends.*

He said nothing. His silence was like a darkness falling over the kitchen, as if someone had closed the plantation shutters. She stopped cutting and turned around slowly, the cleaver in one hand, the hapless fruit in the other, and a gulf of painful emptiness between.

The room wasn't dark, really. Clay stood in a brilliant shaft of clean, white, early-morning sunlight. She could see every detail, from the way wet, curving bits of his dark hair licked at his earlobes to the crisp crease that ran the length of his freshly laundered shirt. He had showered, she thought. He had wasted no time washing away any traces of what had happened in the night.

But the night had left its mark in other ways. Smudges of exhaustion bruised the skin under his eyes. The slight pallor that lurked under his tan told her he was still in pain. His lips were tight, white-edged. A sign of anger? She stifled a craven lurch of fear. Perhaps it was only more pain.

As she studied him, his shadowed gaze met hers, steady and unsmiling.

"Mrs. Hilliard," he said, his voice soft with a gentle menace, the effect intensified by the way he stared at Melanie even while speaking to the other woman, "would you excuse us for a moment? I need to talk to Melanie alone."

To Melanie's amazement, the housekeeper didn't seem to notice the heavily charged atmosphere. Sighing, she nudged a copper jelly mold an inch to the right, bringing it into proper alignment, and then swept past Melanie with only a slight shudder of distaste at the sight of the melon. Pausing in front of Clay, she patted his cheek.

"Fine," she said, her tone no more or less irascible than usual, "but unless you like pureed cantaloupe, you're not going to get any breakfast out of that one. And you could use some sustenance. You don't look as if you're feeling very good." She frowned. "You're not sick, are you? Did you sleep all right?"

Melanie dropped the meat cleaver. Suddenly her fingers simply lost their grip on the handle. The blade bounced off the rubber tips of her sneakers, clattered across the floor and skidded to a halt just inches from Clay's soft leather boat shoes, where it lay glinting in the sunlight. Staring at it, Melanie discovered that she couldn't quite breathe.

"See? I told you that girl is dangerous," Mrs. Hilliard said with a grim satisfaction. "She'll probably try to feed you a doughnut next—if she can't hack up your arteries, she'll settle for hardening them. Hope your willpower's set on high this morning."

Was it Melanie's imagination, or did the pale line around Clay's lips grow even whiter? "Thanks for the warning," he said. "I'll try to resist."

"Humph. Haven't met the man yet who could say no to refined sugar." The housekeeper transferred her glare to Melanie, but to her surprise a twinkle seemed to lurk beneath the scowl. "Especially if it's wrapped up in a pretty little package."

On any other morning, Melanie might have tried to analyze that twinkle—had it always been there? Had the angry, orphaned Melanie of long ago merely been too insecure, too busy tending the chip on her shoulder, to see it? But today there was no time for such musings. Mrs. Hilliard was already stomping out of the kitchen, muttering to herself about men and their sweet teeth.

And suddenly Melanie was alone with Clay.

She set the melon down carefully. He didn't speak at first, and while she waited for him to break the ominous silence, she poured out a cup of coffee, shook three aspirin into her palm and finally extended both cup and medicine toward Clay with hands that she hoped weren't shaking.

He eyed the pills. Lifting one brow sardonically, he gave her a half smile. "I take it you already know about the little man with a jackhammer inside my skull."

She nodded. "I thought you might have a headache."

He made a sound that might have been laughter, perhaps reacting to the understatement. But he didn't say anything. She knew he'd never complain about pain—she'd seen that last night. With one long swig, he knocked back all three aspirin at once. She winced, thinking how the just-brewed coffee must have burned his throat, but he didn't even blink. The shadows under his eyes just deepened by one shade, and a pulse worked heavily in his jaw.

"So how many pills *did* you give me last night, Melanie?" His attempt at clinical curiosity didn't quite work. She could hear the bitter note underneath. "My symptoms this morning suggest that you might have exceeded the recommended daily dosage."

She felt herself standing straighter, as if his disapproval were a wind against which she must brace herself. She tried to recall why sneaking him the medication had seemed so sensible last night, why she had ever thought this man would tolerate being deceived. Still, her motives had been pure; surely he could see that.

"Yes," she admitted as calmly as she could, remembering her vow not to whine or rationalize. "The doctor prescribed one pain pill, but I ground up two of them and dissolved them in your drink."

He stared at her for a long moment, then, suddenly, like an explosion of long-repressed anger, he cursed. "But why, damn it? Why?" He ran his hand through his hair as if he'd like to tear it out. His hands, she thought brokenly. His wonderful hands, so tender last night, so rough this morning. "I told you I didn't want them. I told you I didn't dare—" He shook his head, clipping the sentence off abruptly.

"But, Clay, you were in so much pain—"

"I didn't give a *damn* about the pain." He squeezed his eyes shut hard, touching his thumb and forefinger against the bridge of his nose. "And then to come back in the middle of the night, dressed like that..." He opened his eyes again, and the fire in them was frightening. "Good God, Melanie, why would you do such a stupid, dangerous thing? Surely you knew it could only lead to disaster!"

That was too much. She was willing to bear the guilt, to endure his anger. But she wouldn't stand there and let him talk about the most miraculous experience of her life as though it had been a plane crash or a nasty plunge in the stock market. A *disaster*?

She lifted her chin. "I'm sorry," she said, "but it didn't feel like a disaster to me. It was actually quite wonderful. Perhaps you don't really remember what we—"

"I remember enough," he broke in rigidly. "I remember that you and I, who should never have so much as touched one another, had uninhibited, unwise—and, I might add, *unprotected*—sex on your uncle's library sofa."

She flushed, but somehow she kept her chin at a self-respecting angle. "Then perhaps you can also remember that, while perhaps it wasn't planned, it was still very special. That it was warm, and real, and—"

He took her arm in fingers that were so tight she flinched. "And a violation of every ethics law on the books. *That's* what I remember, Melanie. You're thinking about how it *felt*. Well, I can't argue with you there. It felt fabulous—it was damn near perfect. But a lot of things that feel fantastic are morally reprehensible. For me to have made love to you last night was wrong, dead wrong. Don't you understand that even now?"

She stared at him, suddenly empty inside. She shook her head slowly. "No," she said, "I guess I don't. And to tell you the truth, I don't think I ever will. If that's what it takes to be considered *mature*, then I'm afraid I'll never meet your requirements, Clay. You might as well start distributing Uncle Joshua's estate to the charities right now."

For an instant, his grip tightened almost to the point of real pain. Then, with a harsh, unintelligible syllable, he suddenly released her. And she realized, humiliatingly, that she would rather be touched in bitter frustration than not touched at all.

Taking a deep breath, he moved away from her and, leaning back, propped the heels of his hands against the white marble countertop. He looked so tired, she thought. When he stepped out of the sunbeam spotlight, he looked so terribly tired.

"I almost wish I could," he said flatly. "Unfortunately it's not going to be that easy. After what happened last night, no decision of mine—for *or* against you—would stand up to even the simplest challenge. I'm compromised beyond repair. I've already placed a call to another lawyer, asking him to take over as executor of your uncle's estate.''

"What?'' She couldn't believe what she was hearing. "You're stepping down?''

"Yes. As soon as I can find someone else to take over, which won't be easy.'' He smiled grimly. "Lawyers hate these lose-lose situations.''

"But, Clay...'' She hardly knew what to think, much less what to say. She'd never felt very confident that Clay Logan, elegant paragon of self-control, would ever hand over the Romeo Ruby to the impulsive, whimsical Melanie Browning—but at least she'd learned that Clay was kind, honest, scrupulously fair. At least that had given her a fighting chance. What other ambitious lawyer would contemplate, even briefly, the idea of antagonizing all those blue-chip charities and their powerful CEOs?

Besides, how could Clay so easily relinquish their one excuse for staying together? The thought that he would pass her future over to another lawyer as if she were merely the prop in a game of "hot potato'' was surprisingly painful.

"Clay, you can't. You wouldn't.'' She held out her hands palms up in entreaty. "Why should you? Last night—well, all right, last night was a mistake, I can see that. But there's no real damage done, is there? It's not as if anyone knows what happened. No one knows, don't you see? No one but you and me.''

His expression didn't alter. He might have been made of marble himself. "What more does it take? I know. And you know. That's quite enough to do all the damage in the world, don't you think?''

She felt her cheeks flame. "What exactly does that mean? Do you actually think that *I* would tell anyone? That I would ever use what happened last night against you? Surely you don't think that's why I—''

A strange noise interrupted the flow of her fury. She was

so caught up in the current of her own indignation that it took her a moment to recognize the shrill buzzing of the kitchen telephone. She stared numbly at the high-tech, four-line instrument from which Mrs. Hilliard ran the entire household—and from which, Melanie had always presumed, the housekeeper had by eavesdropping learned the information she needed to thwart Melanie's elopement. The machine buzzed again, as machines do, insisting that it be answered, no matter what else was going on in the world. Even if someone's world was falling apart...

Clay lifted the receiver. Melanie listened—what else could she do? But she couldn't tell who had called—and didn't much care. Clay's responses were curt, and with each passing syllable, his voice dropped lower, grew darker. Several times during the conversation, he referred to an unnamed "him". "Who was with him when it happened?" Clay asked. And later, "Did you ask him why he did it?"

Melanie's chest tightened, and a vague sense of alarm began to seep into her, winding its way through the thick rivers of emotions that already clogged her senses. Belatedly she began to wonder. Who was it? Whom were they talking about?

It was a short conversation. Finally, after promising the caller that he would pass the information along to Melanie immediately, Clay hung up.

"I'm sorry, Melanie, it's Nick," he said without preamble. "He's in trouble."

Melanie caught at the edge of the counter, jarring one piece of the quartered cantaloupe from its wobbly perch and sending it splatting to the floor. Seeds and pulp and juice spread across the white ceramic tiles, but she ignored them.

"What kind of trouble? Who was that? Why didn't you let me talk to them?"

"It was the camp director," Clay said, his voice calm but somehow even more alarming than before. "He didn't ask for you. He just began yelling without asking questions. He was so angry he was practically incoherent, and frankly he's got good reason to be." Clay took a deep breath. "Apparently last night, Nick and some of the other boys stole his car and wrecked it.''

''Oh, my God.'' Melanie's stomach churned. ''Are they all right?''

Clay laughed shortly. ''They're fine, but it seems the car is at the bottom of a ravine, minus a few parts. He says it was Nick and four other campers—and he's expelling them all today. He wants to put them on the next plane out of town.''

''Oh, no.'' Melanie knew she ought to say something intelligent, but she couldn't think what. ''Oh, poor Nick. What on earth got into him? God, he must be terrified.''

Clay's brows drove together. ''He *should* be. But he's probably not. He doesn't have enough sense to be terrified, the damn fool. The director hasn't even called the police, says he doesn't want any adverse publicity for the camp. He says if the parents will just pay for the damage and come get the boys, he'll let them go free.''

''Thank God for that, at least,'' Melanie breathed. Her mind was already racing ahead, wondering how much it would cost to change the airline ticket. They had bought a supersaver fare, which wasn't refundable, and probably there would be some fee—

''What do you mean, 'thank God for that'?'' Clay sounded furious, and she looked up in shock. ''Damn it, you ought to let the man call the police—no, you should *insist* that he call them. It would do that boy a world of good to spend a couple of hours in jail.''

She drew back, horrified. ''You can't mean that,'' she said shakily. ''You can't believe that a fifteen-year-old boy should actually—''

''You bet I do,'' Clay interjected coldly, and she stared at him, bewildered. ''If you let him get away with this now, what kind of message does that send? Stealing a car is a felony, you know. If he does it again when he's eighteen, he won't be spending a few hours in jail. He'll be spending a few *years*.''

''I know,'' she said miserably. ''And I'll punish him. I won't let him get away with it. But jail...''

She struggled to make him understand—but how could she?

He didn't really know Nick—and he didn't have a jot of sympathy for the protective love a big sister could feel for her troubled little brother. Nick in jail? Over her dead body.

She tried again. "Nick's a good kid, Clay, really he is, and this isn't at all the kind of thing he'd do unless he'd been pressured into it by someone else."

Clay made a fist on the counter as if he could hardly hold back his frustration. "Jesus, Melanie, don't you even hear yourself? Who cares who pressured him into it? That's no excuse for committing a crime. Or rather, it's the classic excuse of spoiled delinquents and their softhearted parents who haven't ever forced them to take responsibility for their own actions."

She heard the abstract truth of his words—if this were a debate, he would win it. He was watching her, and she could feel him willing her to understand, to agree. Waves of vehemence pulsed from his long, hard body. He wanted her to see the light, to admit that he was right. He was waiting for her to pick up the telephone and call the camp director, insist that the police be brought in.

"Melanie," he said again, "don't be so shortsighted. Think of his future. It's joyriding today. Tomorrow what will peer pressure push him into? Drugs, booze, sex, suicide? Damn it, how is he ever going to learn to *say* no if he never *hears* no?"

True, she thought, suddenly very sad. Technically it was all true. But as much as she longed to please Clay, to avoid this final confrontation, she simply couldn't do it. This wasn't a debate over parenting philosophies. This was real life. Abstract truth wasn't enough. There was a larger truth here, a messy, human, emotional truth, and it told her that Nick was fragile, bereft over the death of his uncle, the only father figure he'd ever known, more in need of love and security than lessons in discipline.

Nick didn't quite trust her guardianship yet—she could sense that. And with good reason. In Nick's mind, Melanie had abandoned both Nick and Joshua years ago—and he was always testing her, checking to see if there were limits to her love and protection. He was just a lonely, frightened kid, an orphan who wasn't sure he was wanted anywhere.

She knew exactly how that felt.

So...no. No matter how angry it made Clay, Melanie knew she would have to handle this herself. Her way.

"I'm sorry," she said quietly. "I can't. I can't put him through that."

He stared at her. "This is a mistake, Melanie," he said slowly. "A bad one."

"You may be right," she admitted. "But I have to do what my heart tells me, Clay. I can't change who I am—I couldn't do it for Joshua, and I can't even do it for you."

His gaze searched her face as if he was looking for a sign, a glimmer of hope that she could be persuaded. But obviously he found nothing. Something, some spark, flickered and died behind his eyes. He slowly shook his head as though he lamented that little death.

He didn't speak. Kneeling down, he carefully picked up the meat cleaver and the tortured cantaloupe. He placed the fruit in the sink and then stiffly turned back to her. "You started to ask me something a little while ago," he said, his voice a low monotone that reflected the emptiness behind his eyes. "You wanted to know if I believed that our making love was part of a scheme you had hatched to compromise me, to force me to turn over Joshua's estate."

She waited, her senses strangely dulled. She wasn't sure it mattered anymore what he thought about last night. If having casual, unprotected sex with a half-conscious partner wasn't enough to destroy her in his eyes, her decision about Nick certainly was. Taken together, her actions over the past twenty-four hours had obviously demolished any chance that he would declare her "mature" enough to inherit.

"Well, for what it's worth, I don't think you set me up." He jammed the cleaver into the cantaloupe with one hard thrust. Then he moved away, heading toward the kitchen door. At the threshold, he paused. The ghost of a smile brushed his lips. "You *couldn't* have planned what happened last night," he said dryly. "Or any other night, for that matter. It isn't in your nature to think that far ahead."

Ten days later, Melanie parked her Honda in the front lot of the Rolling River Ranch, gave the hood a pat to remind the sputtering engine not to die, then wandered off in search of her little brother, who should have been knee-deep in horse manure by this time.

It was almost noon, and the sunshine lay thickly along the rolling green hills as if they had been buttered. In the middle distance, horses cantered playfully in the paddock, chasing each other like children at recess. Much closer, a drunken bee made a crash landing into a gigantic pink peony.

Melanie smiled. Just a little. The movement felt rusty—it had been a long time since she'd felt like smiling.

Ten days, in fact.

But who was counting? She forced a second smile, determined to loosen the hinges of her mouth. Ten days was long enough to mope and mourn, especially for a man who gave her absolutely no hope. In the entire time, Clay had not spoken to her once. He had hardly set foot inside Cartouche Court. Perhaps he was still combing his Rolodex, looking for a lawyer who owed him a really big favor.

Whatever he was up to, he had been avoiding Melanie as if she were radioactive. The message couldn't have been clearer, and as the painful days passed, she had slowly graduated from guilt and misery to something more akin to anger.

Damn it, she hadn't been the only sinner in the library that night. He had the right to deny her the inheritance, of course, but he didn't have the right to stomp all over her heart while he did it. She had had sex. Just sex. She hadn't murdered anybody. Yet.

Yeah, she was mad. And she was finally ready to do something about it. Ten days of playing the tragic heroine was enough. No more Ophelia bedecked in weeping garlands of wildflowers. No more Hester Prynne shamed by her scarlet letter. No more imperiled Pauline tied to the railroad tracks.

Love wasn't the only reason for living—or for smiling. It

wasn't even the best reason. She had other responsibilities, too, other relationships, other pleasures. Above all, she had Nick.

So to heck with sackcloth and ashes. It was time to act.

She found Nick quickly, which didn't surprise her. Ever since returning in disgrace from camp, Nick had been as easy to locate as if he'd been on a leash. He was always exactly where he should be, doing exactly what he'd been told. Mostly he was right here at the ranch, at the job Ted had found him, grooming horses and mucking out stalls from dawn to dusk.

Today Nick was brushing a dappled brown. Obviously unaware of Melanie's approach, Nick was whispering to the mare, his strokes long, gentle, attentive. Melanie had to steel her heart against the pathos of the skinny, shirtless teenage torso bent tenderly over the shining, muscular flanks of the horse. It was good for him, she reminded herself. By the end of the summer, he'd understand that he had taken the most expensive ten-minute joyride in history.

Melanie couldn't remember ever having seen real sweat— working sweat, as opposed to skateboarding sweat—on her brother's brow before. It looked good on him. And those just might be the beginnings of some grown-up muscles in his shoulders.

The shadows shifted, and across the length of the stable she saw Ted ambling toward them. Good old Ted, looking out for Nick just as he had always looked out for her. It was like having a guardian angel. She was very lucky. She needed one.

As he reached them, Ted grinned at her, cocking his blond head toward Nick, sharing their protective pleasure in his improved attitude. He patted the boy's shoulder as he passed, and Nick smiled an easy greeting.

He liked Ted, Melanie thought. That was important. That would help....

Her heart sped up a little as she remembered the real reason she had come here today. It wasn't just to play Florence Nightingale to an exhausted Nick with her meat loaf sandwiches and diet colas. No, the real reason was Ted. Suddenly she could hardly look him straight in the eye, wondering if he could sense her frayed nerves.

Early this morning, at the raw end of another sleepless night, she'd finally come to a decision, perhaps the most profound decision of her life. In about fifteen minutes, if Ted was willing, her whole future could be altered. She squeezed the rumpled edges of the sandwich bag in her fist and prayed that she wasn't making a mistake.

"Hi, cowboys," she said. She waved the sandwiches at eye level. "Hungry?"

Nick whooped with delight, threw down the grooming brush and made a lunge for the bag. Even Sunny's beloved Blitzen couldn't compete with a growing boy's insatiable appetite for meat loaf sandwiches and potato chips.

Ted simply nodded. "If it's your meat loaf, I am." As Nick headed to stretch out under the shade of his favorite tree, Ted put his arm around Melanie and guided her toward the picnic tables. "Let's sit over here, where we won't interrupt his daydreams of blond cheerleaders, riding bareback to rescue the slave boy from his cruel tormentors."

Good idea, she thought. It was almost as if Ted intuited her need to talk to him alone. Now if she could only work up the courage to say what she had to say.

As Ted unwrapped the sandwiches, the tangy scents of mustard and onion floated toward her, mingling with the odors of horse and hay. When he clicked open the first soda can, she jumped at the sharp, fizzing hiss.

He squinted to get a better look at her. "A little jumpy today?" he asked mildly. "You look pretty whipped. Aren't you sleeping right? Surely a five-star mansion like Cartouche Court hasn't got lumpy beds."

She sipped at her cola. "It's not the mattresses," she said. "You know I'm not the princess-and-the-pea type." That much was true. Her most blissful sleep at Cartouche Court had been a couple of stolen hours on the library sofa.... She fiddled with the aluminum top. "It's just that I have a lot on my mind."

Ted looked sympathetic. "Of course you do. But Nick's doing great. Kid works like a slave all day, they tell me. Has the Grand Executioner been out here to see that for himself?

Surely even he has to admit that you've handled the problem quite well.''

She shook her head. ''Not in a million years,'' she said. ''Clay's already got his mind made up about me. He thinks I'm too shortsighted to make a good decision about what to eat for lunch, much less what to do with a small fortune. All that's left is for him to find some other legal patsy to make the decision official.''

Ted cursed. ''Lousy judgmental bastard,'' he said, his indignation obviously heartfelt. ''Is there really nothing you can do?''

''Well, there is one thing.'' She set down her can of soda, closed her eyes and took a deep breath. ''That's why I'm here, Ted. I came here to ask for your help.''

''Anything, Mel,'' he said softly. ''You know that. All you have to do is ask.''

''You may regret saying that.'' She opened her eyes. ''Because I am asking. I'm asking you to marry me.''

CHAPTER TEN

Two hours later, long after Nick had finished his last sandwich, sighed heavily and dragged himself back to work, Ted finally said yes.

Melanie dropped her head onto her hands and fought back sudden, exhausted tears as relief coursed through her. "Oh, Ted," she whispered to the tabletop. "Thanks. I promise you won't regret it. I'll try to be a good..." But the tears wouldn't let the last word come out.

Ted touched her knuckles with his fingertips. "Hey. The whole point was to make you *happy*." He made a small, wry sound. "And I'm not sure this charade is going to fool anybody if you start bawling every time you try to say the word 'wife'."

She laughed shakily. "Sorry," she said, looking up and brushing the foolish moisture from her lashes. "I really am very tired. And I was so afraid you'd say no."

Smiling, Ted touched her chin lightly. "I'd like to meet the man who could say no to this face. Then I'd want DNA proof the guy is human."

Gratitude welled in her breast—she knew that Ted wasn't just mouthing sweet nothings to cheer her up. Though she had tried to make the deal as attractive to him as possible, she knew he had agreed primarily out of affection and deep, loyal friendship.

Not that the other considerations weren't tempting. Ted would have been insulted by an offer of cash—and besides, buying a husband outright obviously would have violated the terms of Joshua's will—so Melanie had suggested something even better. She had offered to turn Cartouche Court into a boys' academy and give Ted a long-term lease at the perfect price. Ninety-nine years, at a dollar a year.

It was a good deal, especially since the lease would outlast the marriage by about ninety-six years. Though she knew it was a lot to ask, she had told Ted she needed a three- or four-year commitment to making a family for Nick. Technically, of course, it was her choice of husband, not the longevity of the union, that had to be approved by her uncle's executor, but Melanie was determined to keep a normal home intact at least until Nick turned eighteen.

For Melanie, the decision to marry wasn't just about rubies and gold anymore. It was about Nick. The next few years were going to be rocky ones as Nick tried to cross the dangerous gulf that separated boy from man. If she was going to raise her impetuous, misguided brother successfully, she needed more than money. She needed a partner. More the point, she needed a man. A man would understand what adolescent boys went through. A man could provide a role model, an authority figure, a sympathetic ear. And Ted, darling Ted, was the perfect choice.

He had all the right qualities. He was sensible, honest and intelligent. Better still, after all these years as dean of boys, he understood the male teenage psyche better than any therapist. He was genuinely fond of both Melanie and Nick, and she was confident that he would treat them with unfailing respect. And he'd easily pass what Melanie had come to think of as Uncle Joshua's Romeo Test. He was mature, well respected, gainfully and steadily employed. He fell just short of qualifying as wealthy himself, but he was comfortably self-sufficient. All in all, he couldn't be accused of having any personal agenda, of harboring an unhealthy lust for the Browning fortune.

And, amazingly, he wasn't already attached to someone else.

She hoped.

"Ted," she began tentatively, wondering how to broach such a sensitive subject. "There is one thing we haven't talked about." She gazed across the paddocks toward the hills, reluctant to meet his gaze. "We haven't talked about Sheila."

She felt him grow very still. When he didn't answer, she looked over at him. He, too, was studying the horizon. A light wind lifted shining blond strands of hair and feathered them around his forehead. For a moment, his gentle face was as stony and expressionless as Clay Logan's harsher visage, and she shivered.

"I know Sheila's been gone a long time. But if you're still...I mean, I wouldn't want to stand in your way if you think she might..." She sighed, frustrated with herself for beating around the bush. "If you haven't really quite given up hope."

Finally relaxing into a small smile, Ted took her hand. "Trust me, Mel. I've definitely given up hope. She's been gone more than a year, you know. She's probably married herself by now. She made it pretty clear she'd never marry me since I didn't have enough ambition to quit Wakefield and start a school of my own." He raised his brows. "Kind of ironic, huh? If we really turn the Court into a school, I mean."

She nodded. "Yeah. Ironic." She felt ready to strangle the absent Sheila all over again, as she did every time Ted talked about the woman. What kind of ruthless hussy would break this decent man's heart?

Ted squeezed her fingers lightly, summoning her attention. "However, as long as we're on that subject, there's one more thing we haven't discussed," he said. "We haven't discussed Clay."

She feigned confusion. "Clay?" She frowned. "What do you mean?"

He sighed, obviously not believing her act for a moment. "I mean exactly what you meant when you asked me the same question. Have *you* given up hope?"

She began to protest, but one look into his gentle brown eyes told her it was futile. He knew her too well. She let the bluster die on her lips.

"Completely," she said. "It didn't quite qualify as hope anyhow. It was only a dream." She smiled sadly. "Just a little illusion I created with moonlight and medicine."

Clay stared at the pile of "while you were out" memos on his desk and decided there was nothing on earth more boring than estate law. If he had to explain to one more client what a vested remainderman was, or how to set up an inter vivos transaction, he'd probably jump out the window.

Maybe he should have gone into criminal law. Murderers might not be any more noble than overbearing fat cats who tried to control their fortunes from six feet under, but they would indubitably be more interesting. Or maybe he should simply have made a U-turn at the law school gates and gone sailing instead.

He stared across his desk at the eighteenth-century map of the Atlantic Ocean that hung above his bar. Maybe he should do it now—buy a lazy old hound dog and a gleaming new wooden yawl and head for open seas. A man's dreams were more peaceful when he slept alone under a sky full of stars. Or alone anywhere.

Growling, he wadded up the phone memos and lobbed them into the trash. Tracy could retrieve them later if they were really important. He was going sailing.

But even as he thought it, he knew it wouldn't work. He could sail to Timbuktu and back. Hell, he could sail to Timbuktu and *never* come back. But his memories of that night with Melanie would sail right alongside him, like his shadow, like the wind in his hair, like the salt in the air he breathed.

For the first time in his life, he understood what the term "flashback" really meant. It was unnerving as hell. As if he were a brain-fried flower child, he'd have these moments, moments that leaped on him without warning, knocking him to the ground, slamming the breath right out of him. He'd be sitting here at his desk, reading up on trusts or drafting a codicil when *wham*! He'd be back in the library. Melanie's moon-pale body would be above him. And his hands would start to sweat.

It was damned inconvenient. He'd be eating lunch with a client, and suddenly he'd lose track of the conversation. He'd feel Melanie's hands against his skin, her legs trembling around his hips. Yesterday the waitress had to ask him three times if he wanted more coffee before he heard her.

Nothing had ever quite hit him like this before. It must have been the drugs. The whole encounter had been like a series of disjointed, half-conscious physical stimuli. And everyone knew that subliminal messages were the most powerful. Your guard was down—your emotional security system was disabled, so to speak. Anyone could come right in. All the way in. In so deep you could never dig them out again.

But he *had* to. He opened his address book and started again with the A's. He'd been considering and rejecting lawyers for ten days now, trying to find the right one to take over the Melanie Browning mess. But who? Meecher was too greedy— he'd bleed the estate dry. Evangelista was too ambitious— she'd judge Melanie unfit to inherit just so he could lick the boots of the National Research Foundation. Bowington was too old—he'd be horrified by Nick. Dillard was too handsome—he'd probably try to...

Clay cursed, realizing where his thoughts had been going. Was he crazy? Had two lousy prescription pain pills actually made him lose his mind? So what if Dillard made a play for Melanie? Dillard's ethics were his own problem.

He thumbed the speaker button on his telephone hard. "Tracy. Get Jake Dillard on the phone for me ASAP."

Laughter wafted across the airwaves—sweet, silly laughter so like Melanie's that he suddenly felt a little dizzy. Another blasted flashback? It was achingly familiar, so like her, so uninhibited and spontaneous. His heart hurt at the sound of it. She might really have been in the next room.

He squeezed his eyes tightly shut and shook his head, trying to jar the delusion loose. For God's sake, he was going to have to pull himself together here, or they'd be measuring him for a straitjacket pretty soon.

But the laughter came again, a low ripple that carried the exact note of irreverence and lighthearted mischief. It *was* Melanie. He couldn't be that crazy.

He stood, traversed the office in three steps and flung open the door to the lobby. And there she was, on her knees, crawling around under Tracy's desk.

"Mr. Logan!" Eyes widening, Tracy stood at attention.

A small, dismayed sound preceded a loud thump. "Ouch."

The voice under the desk was muffled. "Damn it." And then Melanie's small, rounded bottom wriggled toward him as she backed out from her awkward hideaway.

Flashback. He gripped the frame of the door so hard the paint seemed to soften and yield under his fingertips. *Stop it, damn it. Stop it.*

While he was giving himself a mental shaking, Melanie had clambered to her feet and was busily adjusting the lapels of the most uptight navy blue suit he'd ever seen. He frowned. Why the hell was she dressed like that? He remembered the soft flowered dresses foaming over her furniture. He'd be willing to swear there hadn't been a single one of those iron-maiden suits in the room. She'd probably borrowed it from Mrs. H.

"Hello, Clay," she was saying stiffly. Her hands were working on her hair now, trying to stuff a long, gleaming strand back into the spinster's knot at the nape of her neck. She was having little luck. "Tracy lost her contact lens. She couldn't move an inch or she'd step on it. Luckily I came in and I said I'd help her find it. I didn't, though." She looked around the floor pointlessly. "I'm not sure where it is."

"It's on her collar." He nodded toward Tracy, whose hand flew up to seek the little blue circle that lay on the lacy collar like a shiny button.

"Oh." Tracy grinned sheepishly. "Whoops."

He turned his gaze back to Melanie, whose attempts at fixing her hair had left the whole thing more disheveled than ever. She was biting her lower lip, worrying away all the lipstick she had obviously applied with extreme care.

He fought an overwhelming urge to smile. Poor Melanie. Even when she tried to masquerade as an old-maid librarian nun, she failed miserably. She just couldn't resist the urge to do something impulsive, like crawl around under desks or don a knight's helmet—and the disguise simply wouldn't stick.

"Tracy was just consulting your appointment book," Melanie said formally, lifting her chin in that way he'd come to know so well. "To see when you could work me in."

Tracy riffled tentatively through the pages of the book, obviously unsure exactly what her boss wanted her to say. "Well, Mr. Fisk did cancel his four-thirty. You don't have anyone till Mrs. Murphy at five."

He looked back toward Melanie and raised his brows. He'd been so busy trying to handle his visceral reaction that he hadn't thought to consider what on earth had brought her to his office. "We'd have almost an hour, then, before we'd be interrupted. Will that be long enough?"

"It's more than enough," she said meekly. "Fifteen minutes would be plenty."

He stomped on the answer that rose immediately to his lips. No, it wouldn't. If he found himself alone with her, he might take her in his arms again...and then fifteen *hours* wouldn't begin to cover the things he'd want to do to her.

Somehow he managed to keep his face expressionless. Nodding, he held the door to his office open. He could almost see her girding herself, taking a deep breath, making resolute fists half-hidden in her skirt, then propelling herself through the door with a sudden lurch of determination.

What had she come to discuss that could possibly be so intimidating?

Even after he had shut the door behind them, settled himself on the edge of his desk and waved her toward the most comfortable chair, she couldn't seem to relax. She roamed the room restlessly, touching things. When she came full circle, ending inches from his knees, she picked up his glass paperweight, which had a map of the world etched on it, and studied the thing as if she was preparing for a geography exam.

"This is very pretty," she said without looking up.

"Yes," he agreed, "it is." He paused, but she just kept rotating the glass ball in her fingers. "I have some really neat pencils, too. If I'd known you were coming for a tour, I'd have sharpened them."

She set the paperweight down and finally looked at him. Her cheeks were still as flushed as if she'd been too long in the sun. Her eyes were overbright. She looked as though she was running on adrenaline, as if she was either excited or scared to death.

"You know I didn't come for a tour," she said.

"Yes, I know that." He waited. The only sounds were the clock ticking from the mantel across the room and her unnaturally shallow breathing.

"Actually I came because..." She cleared her throat. "Well, I came to tell you..."

Another silence. With a sigh, she turned away and dropped awkwardly onto the chair he had first offered her. Obviously unaccustomed to the tight suit, she didn't seem to know what to do with her legs. She settled for squeezing her knees and ankles together until even her shins seemed to fuse.

He continued to wait though his inner alarms were beginning to ring. He'd seen this high-strung look before—usually on clients who were about to stake everything on one all-or-nothing gamble. Sometimes it took him hours to talk them out of it.

She was chewing her lower lip, which was now pinker than the top one, even though that one still sported lipstick. "I came to tell you something, Clay. I wanted you to know..." She wasn't allowing her spine to touch the back of the chair. She gulped air. "Ted and I are getting married."

Clay almost laughed. He couldn't help it. Melanie and the Milquetoast? Melanie, who roared through life as if it were a Grand Prix straightaway, married to that ever-so-nice, ever-so-normal dean of boys? Impossible.

But his impulse toward laughter was short-lived. Her face tightened with something that might have been pain. Had his reaction somehow hurt her? Surely even she could see what a ludicrous mismatch such a marriage would be.

"I'm sorry you find this funny." Her lips were unnaturally stiff, and the words sounded strange, as if pique were a foreign accent.

He tilted his head, squinting as though that would somehow make her expression easier to read. "You can't be serious," he said incredulously. "You can't really want me to believe that you're going to *marry* that man."

For answer, she lifted her left hand.

How had he missed it? Melanie never wore jewelry. She

spent every cent on her spoiled little brother and had no money left over for frivolities like that. But today she was wearing a diamond ring. A half-carat solitaire, he estimated, illogically irritated by the commonsense look of it. It was exactly the ring he would have expected Ted Martin's fiancée to wear. Not too showy—no vulgar flash that would have made the dean's wife look immodest.

He felt himself scowling. Though he knew it was an over-reaction, he discovered that he hated the ring. Even someone as lacking in imagination as Ted Martin should have realized that Melanie needed sapphires, which would gleam like her eyes. Or rubies, which would throb wild and red like her heart. Never diamonds, for God's sake. Diamonds were too pale for her.

"It's true. Ted and I are engaged," she was saying as she fiddled nervously with the ring, trying to keep it centered. The band was much too big for her finger, as if Ted had bought it for someone else. "You look skeptical. Is it really so preposterous?"

"Yes, it is." Clay tore his gaze from the diamond, forcing himself to look at her face. "Good grief, Melanie. I know Martin's type. He's a Boy Scout. A rule follower. Whereas you can't get within ten yards of a rule without breaking out in a rash."

She knitted her brows together, and her lips tightened. "Well, haven't you ever heard that opposites attract? People compromise when they fall in love—"

"*Love*?" He leaned forward, suddenly hot and tense from his chest to his knees. This time, he did laugh, and the sound was so harsh it surprised him. "You expect me to believe this engagement was prompted by a sudden outbreak of true love? What kind of a fool do you take me for? I'm sure Ted loves the idea of marrying an heiress, but—"

"But he couldn't love *me*?" She shot to her feet as if her body was too rigid with fury to sit. "God, Clay, you sound just like my uncle. And it just so happens that you're wrong. As hard as it might be for you to imagine, Ted cares about me. We're marrying because we care about each other, because we think we'll make a good family together. The money isn't the issue.''

He twisted a smile toward her. ''But you still want it.''

She didn't flinch though her chin tilted in a haughty dignity. ''Yes, I want it.'' She was clearly angry, but surprisingly her voice was growing steadier. Perhaps his perceived insult had somehow moved her beyond caring. ''The inheritance is morally mine, Clay. That money belonged to my parents, and now it should belong to Nick and me. And if you or any of your hired henchmen try to take it away from us, Ted and I will fight you all the way to the Supreme Court. You may sneer at his virtue, but somehow I don't think it will be possible to dismiss Ted Martin as a gold digger.''

This new calm was a dramatic contrast to her earlier agitation. Clay couldn't help being impressed by it. Impressed, and rather unnerved. Could her confidence mean that the engagement was genuine, that the ''love'' was real?

No. Damn it, no. He didn't remember everything about their night together. Sometimes he lay in bed at night scouring his brain, searching for even one more erotic detail. But he remembered this: She had responded to their lovemaking with an incredible passion, a wholehearted surrender that had been physical *and* emotional.

It had not been the act of a woman in love with another man.

''Damn it, Melanie,'' he growled, the memory acting like sandpaper on his psyche, ''if this is a trick, it's not worth it. Whoever looks after Joshua's estate will investigate Ted thoroughly. They'll check his credit record. If he's behind on even one lousy credit-card payment, they'll discover it and they'll rule against you.''

''Fine,'' she said. ''Let them look.''

''They'll want all his financial records. They'll interview his neighbors. If he has a skeleton in his closet, even one petrified scrap of bone, they'll rattle it.''

She was walking toward the door. ''Fine. Do it. He has nothing to hide.''

He rose, his nerves burning. For one insane moment, he

wondered what she'd do if he tried to stop her, if he grabbed her hand and pulled that ring right off her finger.

"They'll want him to sign a prenuptial agreement. A tough one. He'll have to sign away any rights to your assets should there be a divorce."

"Fine," she said again, her hand on the doorknob. "But you'd better hurry. The wedding is three weeks from tomorrow, and this time there won't be any annulment."

The wedding was only thirteen days away. A hundred decisions remained unmade. But at three o'clock on Sunday afternoon, Melanie floated on the soft, air-filled plastic raft across the lightly rocking surface of the pool and tried to concentrate exclusively on how delicious the warm sun felt on her shoulders. Tomorrow would be soon enough to tackle guest lists, order flowers, create menus. And, of course, pick out a wedding dress.

A wedding dress. She shivered uncomfortably as the sun dipped suddenly behind a cloud. Or had it? Opening her eyes, she realized her raft had drifted toward the shadows of the lagoon. The same lagoon where she and Clay...

Reaching down with her hand, she paddled at the cool water until she was safely back in the white-hot glare of sunshine. She sighed and stretched and pushed the lagoon away mentally as well as physically. Yes, this was better. Perhaps she'd even sleep a little.

But the others were far too noisy for that. Ted and Nick were on the pool deck, engaged in a game of Ping-Pong. Sunny was sitting on the pool steps, humming and splashing her feet, trying to work up the energy to get in the water. And over in the far corner of the patio, Nick's boom box blared. The announcer was whipping himself into quite a lather about the thrills to be experienced at an upcoming monster-truck rally.

All in all, a fairly chaotic, delightfully normal weekend afternoon in suburbia. This was what it was all about, Melanie thought, lulled by the rocking water and the summer sun. They even sounded like a family, didn't they?

She peeked at the ring on her left hand and tried to appreciate the blue and green sparks that flashed in the dazzling sunlight. It had seemed sensible for Ted to give her the same ring Sheila had returned to him a year ago. Why should he spend more money when it was simply a business deal anyhow?

A small white bullet suddenly slapped the water next to her. Smiling, she scooped up the bobbing plastic ball and tossed it back to the boys, who barely managed an apologetic grin before digging into the next point.

She and Sunny exchanged a wry smile.

"It's a hormone thing," Melanie said, sighing. Sunny nodded sagely. United in their common goal of keeping Nick out of trouble, the two women had grown quite friendly since his return from camp. Though Sunny was only a child, Melanie found the sense of partnership comforting. Ted had been beautifully supportive, too, and consequently Nick had settled into his new routine quite well.

This could work, Melanie decided with sudden determination. This marriage could be a success if she'd only let it. She just had to stop thinking about wet kisses in cool, shadowy lagoons, banish all thoughts of naked bodies bathed in blue moonlight. She had to concentrate on sunshine and laughter and the small, simple pleasures of friendship and family.

And, God help her, she had to pick out a wedding dress.

"Miss Browning, you know you ought to put on some sunscreen."

Melanie smiled sleepily at Sunny's anxious tone. The girl really did have a bit of the mother hen in her—it made her perfect for Nick, who needed a ton of mothering.

"Really. You're going to be all burned up and peeling at your own wedding if you don't. Your shoulders look pretty bad already."

Melanie raised herself on one elbow. The sunscreen was over by the Ping-Pong table, which seemed, in her current soporific state, to be about a million miles away.

"Hey, boys," she called. "Next time you're between points, could someone toss the sunscreen over here?"

Ted squatted and groped blindly out with one hand without taking his eyes off the game. He somehow found the bottle of lotion and lobbed it toward the pool. "Here you go," he said.

Sunny caught the bottle before it sank. "I'll do your back for you, Miss Browning," she offered.

"Or I will."

Melanie jerked up at the sound of that voice, that deep, dark voice. "Clay?"

She twisted, trying to get a look, and promptly slid off the raft, all awkward elbows and flailing feet. *Double damnation*, she thought as the water closed over her head and rushed up her nose. She absolutely, positively, could *not* catch a break with this man.

She emerged to the sound of giggling and shot a dirty look toward Sunny. Making a grab for the edge of the raft, Melanie blinked the chlorine burn out of her eyes. "Clay," she said, aware that her struggle for dignity would be easier if a hank of her hair weren't dangling right over her nose. "I didn't know you were here." The sun was behind him, so she couldn't read his face. Probably, though, he wore that half amused, half exasperated look she hated. "Did you need something?"

"I came by to talk to you," he said, and his voice didn't reveal anything, either. "Apparently I've chosen a bad time."

Yes, actually it was a terrible time. Clay came to Cartouche Court so rarely these days that she had relaxed her guard a little. Today she was wearing a particularly skimpy bikini in hopes of getting a spectacular summer tan for the wedding. All things considered, she'd just as soon not have to climb out of the water in front of him.

Just her luck, though—Ted took that exact moment to notice something other than Ping-Pong. "No, no, really," he assured Clay, smiling. "You've come at the perfect time. We were telling Melanie she needs to get out of the sun anyhow."

She could just make out the white of Clay's teeth in his silhouette and knew he was enjoying the moment. He squatted, extending his arm. "Need a hand?"

If she had ignored it, if she had dog-paddled all the way

across the pool to exit on the steps, she would merely have looked ridiculous, so she braced her feet against the wall, took his hand and let him pull her free of the water. It was absurdly easy for him, as if he were a cartoon hero and she a mere scrap of a plaything.

When she stood before him, rivulets of water streaming down her bare legs, plaiting clear, shining webs across her naked torso, the urge to dart for cover was so strong it took all her nerve to let him look at her.

And how thoroughly he looked! Unlike Ted, Clay wasn't the kind of man to pretend he didn't notice how revealing her swimsuit was. His gaze slowly devoured every inch of bare skin, from her face to her toes, and the expression on his face was as frankly sexual as anything she'd ever seen. She felt her feet blushing.

"Just let me get my robe," she managed finally. She somehow covered the distance to the loungers, though she was intensely aware of his gaze following her every step of the way. Tying the thick white terry cloth around her waist with a triple knot, she turned to face him. "Let's go inside, shall we?"

Clay picked the library, of course. The way her luck was running, she should have known he would.

The room was bright, the open dome beaming the golden summer sunshine directly onto the sofa like a studio spotlight. Copernicus cursed eloquently at the sight of them, but his heart wasn't in it. When they didn't bother to chastise him, he returned serenely to his work—unknotting the rope that held his plastic rings.

Carefully avoiding the sofa, Melanie sat in the armchair, shoved her hands in the robe's deep pockets and tried not to shiver as the air-conditioning chilled her wet skin.

"Well?" She kept her voice as polite as possible. "What's up?"

Clay had settled himself casually on the arm of the sofa as if it held no awkward significance for him. Perhaps, she thought with a sudden stab of misery, it didn't—it probably hadn't meant all that much to him. But the sight of his body pressing into the soft brown leather triggered a flood of memories that threatened to overwhelm her.

"I wanted to talk to you about Ted," Clay said mildly.

She stiffened, but she adopted a dry smile. "Is that so? What about him? He told me your secretary asked for his financial records and personal references. Have your investigators discovered that he's in debt to the mob? Or did you find out that he's actually Jack the Ripper?"

"Quite the contrary." Clay raised his brows innocently. "He's every inch the saint you said he was. Not a blemish on the man's record, past or present. Healthy savings account, no credit cards, no debts of any kind. Even contributes his fair share to charity." He shrugged. "So obviously he has no ulterior motives here. Ted Martin doesn't need the Browning fortune any more than I do."

"So...?" She ought to be relieved, but something didn't feel quite right. She didn't fully trust the bland tone of his voice. "So what did you want to talk about?"

He smiled. "Actually I came to apologize, to admit I've been too cynical. If his background check hadn't convinced me that he's a gentleman of flawless moral fiber, what I witnessed here today certainly would have."

Her skin prickled; she sensed that they had reached the real purpose of this conversation. "Oh, really? And what did you witness today?"

"The most amazing display of willpower," he responded with a suspicious animation. "I saw a red-blooded male pass up the opportunity to rub lotion all over the body of the woman he adores. The temptation must have been extreme. It's a rather extraordinary body."

She didn't speak. She stared at him, aware of his point but unable to deflect it.

He smiled again. "But I shouldn't have been surprised, because I've seen similar selfless honor from Ted before, haven't I? I've seen you together several times and I can't help noticing how restrained he is. He doesn't sneak kisses behind corners. He doesn't nudge your knee under the table. He doesn't twist your hair around his finger." He eyed her carefully. "In short, Melanie, your fiancé doesn't touch you at all, does he?"

CHAPTER ELEVEN

MELANIE tried to think of a response.

But at that moment, Copernicus finally completed his mission. As his cluster of rings came unknotted, it clattered down from the perch and fell in a tangle on the floor.

"What the hell?" the bird screamed. He glared down at the toy. "Goddamn it!"

Secretly grateful for the interruption, Melanie stood and retrieved the rings. She carefully retied all the knots, then held the toy out toward the perch. Tilting his body sideways, Copernicus lifted one foot to accept her offering on his toe. It didn't seem to occur to him to thank her.

But even Copernicus couldn't provide distraction forever. Clay was still waiting, she knew that. She turned and looked at him gravely. "I'm sure you think it's all very funny," she said. "But there's no need to laugh at us. Just because Ted and I don't make a display of our affection, just because we don't paw one another in public..."

Clay raised his brows. "In private, then, things are different?"

"Completely different," she lied. "Not that it's any of your business, but my relationship with Ted is... It's completely... It's fully..."

"Physical?"

"Yes." She nodded.

"Satisfying?"

"Yes."

"Passionate?"

"Yes. I told you, yes!" She searched for something convincing to add. "He often comes to the Court late at night, after Nick's asleep. That's our time, our private time."

Perhaps, she hoped, because it was true, it would sound persuasive. Ted did come, almost every night. They closeted themselves here in the library, away from prying eyes. But they weren't exploring the pleasures of affianced passion. They were huddled over blueprints, taking measurements, making plans for adapting Cartouche Court into the Cartouche Boys Academy.

"He can hardly bring himself to leave." Technically that was true, too. Sometimes, exhausted, she went on to bed, while Ted let himself out hours later, blueprints rolled lovingly under his arm. She'd never seen him so enthusiastic about anything before. "He stays very late."

"Oh, he does, does he?"

She might have pushed it too far, she realized, gnawing nervously on her lower lip. Clay's eyes didn't believe it. Their soft chocolate brown had deepened to bottomless black, and the lovely golden flecks were like sharp shards of amber glass. Oh, no, he didn't believe it, and her attempt at deceit obviously angered him.

But she couldn't back down now. "Yes," she insisted. "Very late."

"Does he stay all night?" Slowly, deliberately, Clay stood. He reached out and wrapped his fist around the thick knot at her waist. He tugged on the belt slightly, pulling her toward him, exerting just enough force to prove that she was completely in his power. "Because it would take all night, wouldn't it? If he were really in love with you, if he wanted you the way a man ought to want his wife."

"I told you, that's really none of your—"

He didn't seem to hear her. "And when he comes to you, Melanie, how is it?" His knuckles dug into the plane of her stomach as he tightened his grip and drew her closer. "Does he make you feel the way I made you feel?"

She tried to say yes. Damn his ego! But she was caught by those gold-spangled eyes and she couldn't quite manage the lie. She shook her head, a minute movement, which was all she seemed capable of making.

"It's different," she said, as if that understatement could cloak the real truth. Different? As different as sunshine and snow. Ted's friendly, brotherly touch couldn't even be measured on the same scale with Clay's hot, fierce possession.

"You're damn right it's different," he growled. His lips were hard against her ear; his warm breath found its way into her veins. Her knees seemed to liquify, and she tilted toward him helplessly. "It's a farce, your making love to him. It's no good, it's nothing. And you know it."

"No," she whispered.

"Yes." He grazed his teeth along the edge of her ear, and she shivered. "He doesn't touch you, Melanie." Somehow he had worked the knots free and suddenly his fingers were inside the robe, his palms hot against her bare skin. "Even if he puts his hands on you, he doesn't really *touch* you. Not like this."

He slid his hands down, slipping inside her bathing suit, cupping her buttocks and molding her to him, to the rigid contours of his hard body. She moaned as a hot spear of fire caught and spread from the point of contact.

"His hands may touch your skin, but they don't reach all the way down to the deepest parts of you, so far down it hurts." He moved his hips slowly, subtly. Just an inch, just an unendurable inch in each direction—but her whole body throbbed in response, heavy with yearning, swollen with need. "You don't feel it like this, do you, Melanie? *Do you*?"

"No," she murmured thickly, helplessly. "No."

It was all too much. Her nerves were thrumming as if from sensory overload. Clay's hands were hard, his breath hot. Her body was aching, demanding....

In the background, Copernicus had begun to mutter low, meaningless obscenities that could just barely be heard. From outside the library windows, she could hear someone, maybe Nick, calling her name.

"Melanie! Where are you, Mel? Hey, Melanie!"

"Melanie!" Copernicus echoed, his tone peremptory. "Melanie!"

"I have to go," she whispered, feeling ridiculously close to tears. Why had Clay done this to her? Everything that had seemed so clear an hour ago was hopelessly tangled now. "I have to go."

Clay held her fast, his hands splayed across the tender skin beneath her bikini. "Don't do it, Melanie," he said, his voice hard and low. "Don't marry him. You know it will never work."

"Melanie!" Copernicus was sidestepping across his perch, back and forth, back and forth, obviously quite agitated. "Melanie! Jem-farr-leenk..."

Oh, God. The wretched bird had taken on Uncle Joshua's tones again. He was clearly ready to launch into his mysterious Slavic indictment of Melanie and her reckless ways.

Jem-farr-leenk..."

"Don't do it," Clay repeated hypnotically, as if he couldn't hear Copernicus, or the people calling from the pool, or Melanie's own protestations. "You don't love him."

She couldn't bear to hear another word. With a small cry, she pulled out of his arms and rushed headlong toward the library door. At the last minute, she turned, her eyes filling with tears. "Damn it, Clay, what do you know about *me*?" Her voice broke with frustration and fury. "What do any of you know about me?" She whipped around to the parrot, who was still reciting his secret message. "*Shut up, Copernicus!*"

The bird drew back, suddenly silent. He glared at her a moment, then rotated his face to the wall, obviously offended.

"Well, damn," Copernicus muttered as Melanie fled the room. "What the hell."

A week later, Clay couldn't sleep. He'd begun to get a headache at ten o'clock, right in the middle of his lovely dinner companion's staggeringly boring account of the difficulties of finding a decent hairstylist. *Why don't you just let it grow, for God's sake,* he had silently retorted, thinking of Melanie, whose casual spill of chestnut satin was far more flattering anyhow.

By eleven, he'd invented an excuse to take his date home. But though he had changed into jeans and settled comfortably down to authenticating the last of Joshua's most controversial maps—an occupation that usually relaxed him—his headache had just grown worse by the hour.

When the guest cottage ran out of beer at two o'clock, that was the last straw. Barefoot and bare chested, he wandered irritably across the patio and let himself quietly in through the kitchen door of the Court. Mrs H. always kept plenty of beer on hand. Probably knocked back a few herself, he thought, when no one was looking.

Grabbing the nearest can, he popped the top and dragged in a long, serious swig. But his headache didn't subside. He stood for a while, staring into the refrigerator, wondering if Mrs. H. had made any of her killer chocolate cake and rubbing the icy aluminum can against his pounding temple.

He might have stood there forever—at two in the morning a person can be oddly mesmerized by weird things, like Mrs. H.'s elaborate system of dating and color coding leftovers. But a small sound from the direction of the library finally caught his attention.

Who else was up at this hour? Surely not Nick. The boy worked hard these days, and he slept hard, too. Clay scowled. That left two alternatives—a burglar making off with a small fortune in antique maps, or Melanie and her demon lover, Ted Martin. It annoyed the hell out of him to realize that, of the two options, he preferred the idea of the burglar.

He shoved the refrigerator door shut, muttering a curse at his own stupidity. Why the devil did it matter to him? In the week since Melanie had told him about her late-night assignations with Ted, Clay had been absurdly fixated on the topic. Every single night, he'd caught himself inventing excuses to come over to the Court. Every night, he had restrained himself, had hauled himself back by the scruff of his own stupid neck.

Until tonight.

But that was different, he told himself. He'd just needed a beer. He *didn't* care, damn it. Melanie and Ted could make love swinging from the chandelier for all it mattered to him.

But just in case it actually was a burglar, he ought to check. Nick wasn't quite old enough to serve as a bodyguard for the women. Although he reminded himself wryly as he padded across the foyer, any intruder dumb enough to mess with Melanie Browning was going to be one sorry son of a gun. She probably slept with a chain saw.

The noise was definitely coming from the library. It sounded like someone moving furniture. And as he drew nearer, he realized that someone was softly singing the theme from *Oklahoma!* He smiled at the half-closed door. In his experience, few burglars hummed show tunes while they worked. And even fewer sex-crazed lovers.

He almost knocked, but then he changed his mind. Any rap on the door was sure to rouse Copernicus into a storm of swearing. Still, as the charming, off-tune voice was now humming "Singin' in the Rain", Clay felt fairly certain that he wouldn't be interrupting anything intimate. He pushed the door open.

At first, he couldn't see her. Because it was Melanie, he scanned all the strangest places, just in case she was picnicking under the desk or dancing on the rafters. But he saw no one. Her humming had stopped abruptly at the sound of the creaking door, and he realized guiltily that he might have frightened her. Perhaps she was hiding.

"Melanie?" He spoke quietly, remembering Copernicus. "Is everything okay?" Still no answer. He stepped into the room, noticing that someone had dragged a chair over to the library stacks. Sensing movement, he headed toward it. "Melanie?"

When he drew very close, something rustled. He heard a strangely muffled mutter. And then, slowly, with an air of almost melodramatic reluctance, a little green man in a pink flannel suit rose inch by inch from behind the chair. The little man sighed heavily, squared his pink shoulders, then faced Clay as if he were a firing squad.

For a split second, Clay stared, bewildered. The little green man had a thick, glossy sprout of crazy brown hair growing right out of the top of his head, like a Flintstone kid. In his lumpy green face, only two wide white eyes and one gaping mouth could be identified. *Oh, good Lord...* Struggling to maintain his composure, Clay scanned the pink-flannel alien, from the oversize sleeves to the tips of the...the...

Clay laughed out loud. His little green man was wearing pink bunny slippers.

The alien lifted her cute green chin. "Ever heard," Melanie asked furiously, "of knocking?"

"I'm sorry," he managed. "I was in the kitchen and heard someone in here, so I thought I'd better check. I thought..." He was having a hard time talking. Laughter kept wanting to come out instead. He wondered if he was just a little bit drunk. This delightful evidence that she was *not* swinging from the chandelier with Ted Martin seemed to be making him altogether too happy. "I thought..."

He gave up. Putting one knee on the seat of the chair, he leaned forward to get a better look at her. He touched a finger to the green cheek. To his surprise, the lumpy coating was dry.

"Melanie," he said, his throat still tight with repressed laughter, "I'm sorry, sweetheart, but I just have to know. What the hell *is* this stuff?"

"For heaven's sake, didn't you ever have any sisters?" She batted his hand away. "It's a beauty mask."

"A *beauty* mask?" He raised one brow. "No kidding."

"Well, what on earth did you think it was?"

"I wasn't sure." He thought a moment. "I was leaning toward either toxic lava or guacamole dip."

Harrumphing irritably, she edged away from his hand and finally left the protection of the chair. As he watched her walk toward the sofa, he realized that he definitely had had one beer too many. Otherwise he would never have mistaken this alien for a male. The flannel pajamas found her sexy curves and clung to them.

He grinned at the ponytail that bobbed from the crown of her head. Could that tight elastic band be comfortable? He noticed suddenly that his headache was completely gone. Apparently all he'd needed was a good laugh. And Melanie was the perfect tonic—much better than beer.

He smiled again. She really was just unbelievably adorable.

"I take it Ted's not here tonight," he said politely, deciding to have a little fun with her. It seemed like a good night for fun. Maybe later they'd sing tunes from *Annie* together. Maybe she'd dance on Joshua's desk, and he'd watch—

"Ted?" She whisked around, bracing her hands behind her on the table that held Joshua's handcuff collection. Though it was difficult to read her expression under all that goop, he thought she looked nervous. "Well," she said, "well, actually, he *is* here. He's in..." She tilted her head an inch or so toward the adjoining room. "He's in there."

Clay flicked a glance toward the half-closed door. He eyed it skeptically. "He's in Joshua's bedroom?"

"Yes," she said. "He's...he's waiting for me."

He didn't believe it. He grunted, moving toward the other door. "In Joshua's *bedroom*?" He put his hand on the door-knob as if he needed to see this with his own eyes.

"Don't go in there," Melanie ordered hotly. She visibly relaxed when Clay let his hand fall from the brass knob. "Sorry. It's just that he...he might not be decent."

Clay slanted a disbelieving look at her. "What?"

"I said he might not be decent." She toyed with one of the buttons on her pajama top. "You see, he's waiting for me."

She was lying, he thought complacently. He didn't believe that anyone was in that room and certainly not anybody's red-hot lover. But at that precise moment, as if on cue, a loud snoring could distinctly be heard. His eyes widened.

"That's Ted?" He shot a quizzical look toward the harsh, buzzing sounds. He raised his brows. "He must have been waiting a long time."

She frowned hard, obviously unamused. The mask cracked between her eyebrows like a baked green dessert. "Yes, well, I guess I took too long. I was going to change. I was going to put on something more...I was going to..."

He smiled. "To wash your face?"

"Yes."

"But when I came in, you were looking for something here in the library," he said. "There's no sink in here."

"Yes, well, that's true. But you see, Ted wanted me to get

something. He wanted me to get...'' She looked round the room. ''To get...''

He allowed his tone to express polite curiosity. ''Get what?''

As she chewed on the inside of her lower lip, her gaze ricocheted from bookcase to desk, from Copernicus's cage to the sofa. But obviously she found no inspiration. She groped clumsily behind her, grabbing for something... Grabbing for anything, he realized. Anything at all.

She held out her hand triumphantly. ''This!''

He looked down. She looked, too, obviously just as curious as he was.

It was a small pair of medieval thumbscrews.

''Wow.'' He whistled softly. ''Ted sent you to get those? You know, I think I may have underestimated the man.''

Poor Melanie. She couldn't stop staring. She made a small, strangled sound and her shaking fingers opened wide, as if rejecting the thing that lay in her open palm. Even through the thick green mask, he could see her face burning fire-engine red.

By some miracle he managed not to laugh.

''It's all right, Melanie,'' he said sympathetically. He was enjoying himself immensely. He quite admired the precise note of avuncular understanding he achieved. He should have been an actor, he thought. ''Honestly, you don't need to be embarrassed. I'm well aware that young couples often...experiment.''

She was frozen in place, a tableau of horror. But he sauntered over to the small table behind her and studied it thoughtfully. After a moment, he selected a pair of golden handcuffs, the pride of Joshua's collection, and held them up for her approval.

''Maybe you should try these,'' he suggested. ''They're not as exotic, of course—maybe even a little clichéd. But they're probably a lot less painful.''

The noise she made didn't quite qualify as a word. Gently he picked up her other hand and folded the handcuffs into her palm.

"I'll leave you two alone now," he said somberly.

He thought he sounded a little like an undertaker, which made him want to chuckle. At this very moment, she undoubtedly wished she were dead.

At the door, he paused. "Tell you what," he said helpfully. "There's a popular old fantasy game you two might want to try tonight. Do you know it? It's the one about the beautiful alien who abducts the poor earthling to do naughty experiments on him." He kept the door ready to be used as a shield in case she decided to throw the handcuffs at him. "Think how convenient," he added, grinning. "You won't even need to wash your face."

Melanie couldn't decide whether to kill Clay now or to wash her face first. But vanity was stronger than fury, so she stomped into Joshua's bathroom, right past the snoring body of her fiancé, and scrubbed her face until it hurt.

Then, when her cheeks had switched, like a traffic light, from green to red, she pulled her hair out of its elastic band and let it fall around her shoulders. She kicked off the stupid bunny slippers Nick had bought her for Christmas. Why couldn't he have given her a nice, dignified pen and pencil set? No. It had to be bunny slippers. Maybe she'd kill Nick, too.

She might as well add Ted to the list while she was at it. She leaned against the doorway, staring at his recumbent body. How dare he fall asleep? He was supposed to be in here measuring the dimensions of the room, comparing them to the blueprints. But the house plans were spread all over Uncle Joshua's massive walnut four-poster bed, and Ted was snoring away beside them.

Thank heaven she had managed to keep Clay out of the bedroom. The blueprints would have told the entire story. Clay wouldn't even have needed to ask what Ted's ulterior motive for this marriage really was. Clay could have fired all his investigators and saved himself a bundle of money.

Ted shifted in his sleep, rolling over on the crackling papers. She shook her head, disgusted. Yes, definitely, all three of the men in her life had to die. That humiliating scene out there in the library had been the last straw, just absolutely the final blow. *Alien abduction fantasies, my foot! How about Lizzie Borden fantasies? Lucrezia Borgia? Lady Macbeth?* She'd find a use for these blasted handcuffs all right, and the thumb-screws, too.

But right now, as her indignation finally began to recede, she realized she just wanted to go to bed. She wanted to forget about the whole mortifying scene. She knew Clay had just been teasing her, but why had she played so perfectly into his hands? Why was she so incompetent at this madly-in-love charade?

But she knew why. And Clay probably knew why, too. It probably struck him as hilarious. So she refused to let herself brood over it—why give him the satisfaction? If he thought he could just come sauntering in, with his gorgeous bare chest and his strangely sexy bare feet, and try to tell her how to run her love life...

With a resigned sigh, she bent over and began rolling up the blueprints. Wasn't that just like a man, falling asleep and leaving her to clean up the mess?

Ted might have sensed her presence because he muttered and turned over again, but he didn't wake up. In spite of herself, she felt her heart softening at the sight of his sweet, exhausted face. Well, she thought, maybe she'd let Ted live. He couldn't have guessed that he'd be needed to play the role of panting fiancé tonight.

As she tidied the last of the papers, she spied a dark brown wallet lying open on the pillow beside him. She picked it up, prepared to set it safely on the bedside table, but as she did so, a small, well-worn photograph of a woman fell out.

Who was this? Ted must have been looking at it before he fell asleep. And he must have wanted to touch it, too—he'd removed it from its plastic sleeve. Judging by the creases, it wasn't the first time he'd held this little picture in his fingers.

Curious, Melanie studied the face. It was a color photo, fairly recent, of a beautiful blond woman, maybe twenty-five or so, with a brilliant white smile and intelligent blue eyes.

Her graceful hands were folded in her lap, and if Melanie squinted just right, she thought she could make out a small diamond on the woman's left hand.

It wasn't signed, but Melanie knew who it had to be. Sheila Glasgow, Ted's erstwhile fiancée, the woman who had left him brokenhearted a year ago.

Melanie suddenly felt very strange. She stared at her own left hand, where the same small solitaire gleamed in the light from the bedside lamp, then turned back to the picture. So this was Sheila, the woman who had once worn this ring. The woman Ted had said he would never forgive. The woman he vowed he no longer cared about.

And yet he'd been lying here, in the middle of the night, staring at Sheila's picture. Running his index finger across that smile, perhaps. Imagining the feel of her silky blond hair. She looked like a very nice person, actually. Not at all the shrew Melanie had been imagining.

"Ted," Melanie whispered. "Oh, Ted..."

Her heart tightened as she thought of the terrible ways in which people hurt one another. Sheila had broken their engagement a year ago and moved to Los Angeles. Had she hoped Ted would follow her? Had she hoped he would call, find a way to set things right somehow? Melanie knew that Ted had steadfastly refused to do any of those things, determined to hang on to his pride, if nothing else.

Pride. What a dreadful, destructive emotion that was! How many lives could be wrecked, how many hearts bruised and broken, simply because people refused to admit how much they cared? How much they needed other people...?

And all at once, looking down at the touching innocence of Ted Martin's sleeping face, she knew she couldn't do this. Not unless she was sure. Not unless *he* was sure. She couldn't marry Ted if his heart was pining away for another woman.

What about her own pining? a small voice inside asked her. But she hushed the voice quickly. Her situation was different. She hadn't lost Clay Logan because she was too proud to admit her feelings. In fact, in the most vulnerable, openhanded way possible, she had admitted her love for him, had given herself to him, body and soul. And he had declined the gift.

But Ted...Ted was different.

"Don't be mad, Ted," she said, touching his shoulder softly, though she knew he was sleeping. "I have to do this." And then she went out into the library and picked up the telephone on Uncle Joshua's desk. "Information?" she said quietly when she reached the Los Angeles operator. "I'm looking for a woman named Sheila Glasgow."

CHAPTER TWELVE

WHEN the doorbell rang the next afternoon, Melanie put her hand over her chest to keep her heart from knocking a hole through it. She had an amazingly strong premonition that it would be Sheila, returning as requested to claim her fiancé.

Strange, this certainty she felt that Sheila was on her way. Last night, Melanie had reached Sheila's answering machine—she couldn't even really be sure the woman had received the message yet. And yet, somehow, she didn't doubt that the beautiful, blond Sheila would arrive at Cartouche Court sometime today.

She cast a nervous look at Ted, who was in the corner of the library reading a book on private-school management, blissfully unaware of the bomb Melanie was about to drop into his life.

The doorbell ran again.

"Who the hell is it?" Copernicus demanded suspiciously. He glared at Melanie as if he knew she was up to something. She stuck her tongue out at him, and he stuck his out at her, enjoying the new game.

Fighting to keep her breath normal, she listened to Mrs. H.'s footsteps traversing the foyer to the front door. With one hand, Melanie fed sunflower seeds to Copernicus, trying to look innocent and unconcerned. The other, she held behind her back, fingers crossed, praying that Ted wouldn't be furious.

There seemed to be quite a lot of hustle and bustle at the door. She heard several voices, which made her nervous. Had Sheila brought someone with her? Please, not a husband, she prayed. No big, burly, ticked-off boyfriend. Perhaps, she thought ruefully, her complicated message about impending nuptials and dog-eared pictures and the tragedy of misplaced pride had seemed a little wild. Maybe Sheila had brought a bodyguard to protect her from the crazy lady.

171

But it wasn't Sheila. It seemed, in fact, to be everyone in the world *except* Sheila.

Clay entered the library first, followed by another expensively tailored, ridiculously good-looking man. Melanie pegged him immediately as another lawyer. She felt her heart sink—was this the new Executioner? Had Clay really done it—had he really ransomed her to someone else? But her misery was cut short by another numbing shock that came rolling in right behind the men: a smiling, well-coiffed, middle-aged woman pulling a large, wheeled cart filled with...

Wedding dresses.

Melanie's fingers went slack, and a handful of sunflower seeds spilled messily onto the floor of Copernicus's perch. Unable to formulate a sensible thought, she stared helplessly at the cart. At least two dozen wedding dresses—some short, some long, some tailored, some dripping with lace—hung from a silver bar. The ride had set them swaying gently. The whole thing looked like a restless white ocean that had been sprinkled with seed pearls, opalescent sequins and twinkling rhinestones.

"What the hell?" Copernicus apparently spoke for all of them. Out of the corner of her eye, Melanie could see that even Ted looked slightly stunned. He had the same slack-jawed, deaf-mute expression she knew she must be wearing.

"Melanie, I'd like you to meet a couple of people," Clay said. He rested his hand on the shoulder of the other man. "This is Jake Dillard. He's here to discuss taking over as personal representative for your uncle's estate."

The man smiled and extended a hand, which Melanie shook without even feeling it. She revised her earlier assessment. Black-haired, blue-eyed and possessed of two outrageously sexy dimples, Jake Dillard didn't really look like a lawyer. He looked like a movie star playing a lawyer.

"I'm delighted to meet you," he said. "I hope we can work effectively together."

"Yes," she said stupidly. "Yes, I'm sure we can." Whatever that meant. She couldn't bring herself to meet Clay's gaze. She suddenly realized that she hadn't believed he'd ever really do it. *How could you?* she asked him, mutely the question reverberating in her head. She felt absurdly like crying. *Oh, Clay, how could you?*

"And this is Larisa Daveed," Clay continued, as expansive as if he was hosting an immensely successful party. "Mrs. H. tells me that, around here, they say you're not really married if your dress didn't come from Ms. Daveed's salon."

The lovely woman extended her hand with charming dignity. "The man who flatters too much is not to be trusted," she said, slanting a scolding glance toward Clay. Her voice was tinged with a slight foreign accent. "But I will be quite honored, Miss Browning, if I can help you find a dress to make you happy on your special day."

It was all slightly surreal. Melanie heard herself making courteous comments—who could dream of being uncivil to such an elegant lady as Larisa Daveed?—and in the background she heard more introductions going around as Ted was included in the conversation. But it all sounded like meaningless babble. What she heard most clearly was the hollow rush of her own blood in her ears.

Take the dresses away, she wanted to scream. *There will be no wedding. My fiancé and I are both in love with other people.*

But of course she could say no such thing. Jake Dillard was mildly flirting with her while Ted was valiantly trying to look enthusiastic about the idea of Melanie in a wedding dress and Ms. Daveed was expertly analyzing Melanie's shape and style. Clay himself was watching over it all like some deity from Mount Olympus who had just created a terrifically amusing hurricane.

"Okay, Dillard, let's go. We've got work to do," Clay said finally, breaking into the clamor. "And Melanie has a wedding to plan."

Already deep in creative concentration, Ms. Daveed had pulled out a dress and was alternately squinting at it, then at Melanie. It was the most extraordinary gown Melanie had ever seen. Long, full-skirted, antique-white watered silk. Astonishingly plain. No ruches of lace, no salting of rhinestones. Just a wide, low collar and a long, trailing velvet bow down the back. The dressmaker held it up against Melanie, tucking the hanger crisply under her chin.

It must have suited her. Jake Dillard whistled appreciatively, and even Ted looked impressed. Clay was strangely silent.

"Ahhh," Ms. Daveed murmured. "I have been looking very long for the woman who could wear this dress." She flicked the gown away and draped it over her arm in one practiced motion. "Come. I must see it on you." She turned to the men. "Go away. We need privacy. We must have a mirror to the floor."

"How about Joshua's room?" Ted suggested. "It has a full-length mirror."

"Good." The woman smiled at Melanie. "Do not worry," she said, patting her arm softly. "It is not unusual to fear the dress. It represents so much that is to be lost. And yet it also represents much that will be found. The right dress will show you all of this."

A sudden film of tears shimmered in front of Melanie's eyes. She could hardly speak. If she had dreamed a wedding dress, it would have looked like this one. And yet, if she had dreamed a groom, it wouldn't have been Ted.

A loud wolf whistle interrupted her thoughts. "Hey, baby," Copernicus called suggestively. "Lookin' good!" Everyone laughed, which seemed to please him enormously. He strutted across his perch, whistling over and over with an air of self-satisfaction, "Lookin' good!"

Melanie was ready to stuff a sock in the little show-off's mouth, but Ms. Daveed seemed charmed. "This bird," she announced, "has very discriminating taste. This gown is quite subtle. At home in Hungary, everyone loves it, but here..." Rather than insult the American taste, she let the sentence drift off.

Ted grinned. "I hate to disillusion you, but Copernicus has a thing for Melanie. When he saw her in a bathing suit, he nearly fell off his perch."

The dressmaker waved her hand airily. "This does not matter. Look at Miss Browning. I think the bird would still be quite correct, would he not?"

"Well, since you and Copernicus seem to be in tune, Ms. Daveed, maybe you can help us with something," Clay interjected. He plucked Melanie's picture from Joshua's desk. "The bird has a very strong reaction to this portrait, but we don't recognize the words he uses. It's possible he's speaking Hungarian. Listen...''

Before Melanie could even sort out all the wretched implications, he held the photo up for Copernicus to see.

"No..." she cried, a painful sound so low no one heard it. How could he humiliate her in front of all these people? And poor Ms. Daveed—if by some horrible mischance she did recognize the words, she'd probably faint dead away from shock. Melanie wished that she was the fainting type herself. Anything to escape this terrible moment.

But it was too late. At the sight of Melanie's pouting image, Copernicus bobbed eagerly up and down and launched without hesitation into his strange little speech. Melanie thought, almost numbly, that Clay must despise her very much indeed.

Thrilled with his unusually large audience, Copernicus outdid himself. He went through the speech, all eight or ten words of it, without hesitation, and then did it again.

Melanie couldn't look at anyone, couldn't raise her eyes above the tips of her shoes. So she was shocked to hear the delighted bell-like laughter as Ms. Daveed gleefully clapped her hands together.

"I told you this bird is a creature of fine tastes," the woman said. "This bird, this smart little bird, is quoting Shakespeare!"

A murmur of interest circled the room. Melanie looked up and found that Clay's smiling gaze was softly upon her. She shook her head, confused.

"Well, what is he saying?" Jake Dillard asked impatiently. He seemed just as curious as everyone else, though he knew none of the history behind the moment. "Is it 'to be or not to be'? That's about the extent of *my* Shakespeare, and I'd hate to think the bird is smarter than I am."

Ms. Daveed looked thoughtful. She put a graceful, pink-tipped finger to her lips and stared musingly at Melanie. "No," she said. "This is a message for Melanie. I will tell her only." She took a deep breath. "Go now. She may tell you later if she chooses."

No one liked it, but everyone could tell it was no use arguing. Dillard ambled toward the door, though Ted opted to wait in the library reading while the women were using

Joshua's room. Clay stayed behind only long enough to pull a book from the shelf.

He handed it to Melanie. "Page thirty, if I remember correctly," he said without any particular inflection.

She took it in hands that wanted to shake, though she refused to allow it. The book was a blue-leather volume of Shakespeare's sonnets. "You've known all along what Copernicus was saying?" She studied his face, searching for any answer that would make sense of the whole thing. "Why? Why didn't you tell me?"

He smiled. "I didn't think you were ready to hear it."

She tilted her head and asked the first thing that came into her mind. "What makes you think I'm ready now?"

He looked away for a moment. Silently he fingered the silky white sleeve of the nearest wedding dress. When he looked back, his face was unreadable. "I'm not sure," he said quietly. "Perhaps I just think you know a little more about love now." He grazed her cheek with the back of his hand. The touch felt almost sad. "I could be wrong. But I hope I'm not."

"Farewell," the sonnet began. "Thou art too dear for my possessing."

Ms. Daveed let Melanie cry for a while. She even pretended not to notice, though Melanie observed that tissues mysteriously appeared on the bedside table. Diplomatically, the dressmaker busied herself dusting creases out of sleeves and plucking imaginary threads from necklines while Melanie sat on the edge of Joshua's bed, her tears falling into the little book of sonnets like a small, private rain.

Folded into that page was a sheet of paper on which Joshua had written both Shakespeare's line and its Hungarian translation. Just the one line that Copernicus had learned. No explanation, of course—she smiled through her tears at the outrageous idea. Explain himself? Not Joshua Browning.

Still, Melanie believed she understood what he was saying. He knew he had not been kind to her. He hadn't given her the love she had prayed for, the warmth she had so desperately needed. He hadn't wanted children in his house—and yet they had been thrust upon him. He especially had not understood girls, hadn't liked them much. He had hurt her. Badly. And finally she had fled from him.

This, she somehow felt, was his way of saying he regretted that. He was telling her that he understood her flight and that he accepted responsibility for it. Perhaps he was also telling her that he had missed her.

She tried to picture Joshua, sitting alone in the library night after night, teaching Copernicus to say this simple line, holding up her picture, repeating the strange words so that no one who overheard him would ever understand. He wouldn't have endured pity. He wouldn't have wanted the world to know that Joshua Browning suffered regrets over anything he'd done.

He was still the same man after all. One line of poetry didn't change everything like a magic incantation. Joshua had been proud, selfish, full of machismo and snobbery. But he hadn't hated her and he hadn't blamed her for leaving.

She kissed her fingers and touched them to the little folded piece of paper. Somehow, at least for now, that was enough to know.

Standing up, she began to unhook the buttons that ran down the front of her loose, flowered dress. "I'm ready," she said simply.

Ms. Daveed bustled over, holding out the lovely watered-silk gown.

"Very good, very good." She smiled. "I brought many dresses. Mr. Logan said you must have many choices of all my most beautiful dresses. But I do not think so." She held the full skirts up, and Melanie ducked her head under it. They smiled at each other as she emerged. "No, I do not think so," the woman said contentedly. "I think that you will be married in this dress."

Melanie held herself very still as Ms. Daveed adjusted the collar, the bow, the buttons. As much as she hated to disappoint the charming woman, she knew she was going to have to tell Ms. Daveed the truth.

Whether Sheila showed up or not, Melanie would never marry Ted.

She had discovered this truth only moments ago herself. Everything seemed different now. She knew that she could never again consider marrying a man she didn't love. Not, as she had done at sixteen, to hurt her uncle, or just to fill the empty places in her own heart. Not for money. Not even for Nick.

Not for any reason on the face of this earth.

She wasn't really sure what Clay had meant by his cryptic remark, but he had been right: She did know more about love now. She understood that all real love took courage, and she believed that she possessed that courage.

She knew how to love her brother—with discipline, tolerance, frustration and warmth. She knew how to love her friend—with gratitude and loyalty, and offering freedom for each to pursue one's own dream. She knew how to love her uncle—with sorrow untinged with bitterness and, eventually, an openhearted forgiveness.

She even knew how to love a man—with passion and honesty and a full, unguarded heart. And, now that she knew, she would never settle for anything less. Perhaps someday she would be lucky enough to love a man who would love her in return. Till then, there would be no weddings.

She met Ms. Daveed's gaze in the mirror. "I'm sorry," she began. "It's the perfect dress. But I—"

At that moment, the doorbell rang again. She held her breath, feeling her skin flutter with sudden goose bumps. She heard the newcomer...a strange female voice. A flurry of running feet, a door flung open, a book falling to the floor. And then Ted's voice, shocked and full of wonder.

"Sheila?" A low, heartfelt cry, the sound of hope reborn. "My God. Sheila..."

An hour later, Melanie was alone in the library. Ted and Sheila had finally left, hand in hand, misty-eyed and overflowing with gratitude. Ms. Daveed was taking coffee with Mrs. Hilliard, and Clay, she assumed, was still going over details with Dillard. It was the first moment of peace she'd had in days, and she savored the bittersweet silence.

She sat on the sofa, her feet tucked under her, the wedding dress pooling around her on the soft sofa. From the dome overhead, the pale sunset poured down on her like honey from a pitcher, making the white silk gleam wet, warm and golden.

Around the room, stray beams sparkled on the gilt inlay on Uncle Joshua's desk and burnished the gold-stamped titles of row upon row of rich leather books.

What a beautifully designed room this was, she realized, as if she'd never seen it before. It was too bad, in a way, that she hadn't been able to fully appreciate Cartouche Court until now, when it was lost to her forever. Still, she wouldn't regret leaving. She hadn't ever longed for fourteen-foot ceilings and marble statuary. Perhaps someone, even if it couldn't be Ted, would turn the Court into a school after all, and the cold rooms would grow warm with children's laughter.

It all seemed fitting somehow. Joshua's maps would go to libraries, where hundreds of scholars would study and enjoy them. Even the ruby, the infamous Browning Romeo Ruby, would be better off in the hands of the National Research Foundation. It would save lives from now on, not destroy them.

Yes, she thought. She could leave this house and the entire Browning fortune without much more than one wistful backward glance.

But Clay... Clay, the sexiest Grand Executioner ever born to break her heart, was the loss that hurt the most. Honorable, fair-minded, infuriatingly stiff-necked and frightening perceptive, he had taught her more about love and happiness in one month than she had learned in a lifetime without him.

Farewell, she began mentally, thinking how apt Joshua's quote had turned out to be after all. But maudlin tears threatened, and she refused to finish the line. She was lucky just to have known Clay. She would not wallow in self-pity, not even for the length of five iambic pentameter feet.

"Hi there. All alone?"

She turned at the sound of Clay's voice, feeling that familiar rush of warmth at the sight of him. She was pleased, in spite of everything, in spite of the difficult confessions she was going to have to make, in spite of the pain of losing him, that he was here. She was glad that they were finally alone together one more time.

"Hi," she said. "I was hoping you'd come. Can you stay for a little while? So many things have happened. I have a lot to tell you."

Without a word, he entered the room, pulling the door shut behind him. He sat next to her on the sofa, his knee touching white silk, the sunlight gilding his face. His strong, handsome face, she thought. It had become so dear to her that she wanted to reach out and touch it, just for the joy of feeling his warm skin under her fingers.

But now was not the moment for that. Sorrow pinched at her heart as she realized that such a moment would never come again. She would have to make do with memories. And she had so few of those.

"I've got all the time you need, Melanie," he said generously, settling himself comfortably, his arm outstretched along the back, his fingers just millimeters from her shoulder. "Tell me what's on your mind."

She folded her hands firmly in her lap and met his gaze somberly. This confession couldn't be avoided, so she might as well get the worst said first. "Ted and I won't be getting married," she said bluntly. She took a deep breath and looked at him, waiting for his reaction.

"I see," he said noncommittally. "And how do you feel about that?"

"I feel... Well, I guess I should start by telling you the truth about Ted and me. You see, I've been..." She looked down at her hands, preparing herself for his blistering indictment of her morals, her character, her judgment. "I've been deceiving you."

"No," he said calmly, "actually you haven't."

"Yes, I have," she insisted. "I've been lying about.." Belatedly she understood and, flushing, looked up at him miserably. "Oh, I see. You weren't deceived, you mean."

He raised his brows and shook his head apologetically. "Not for a minute."

He didn't look at all disturbed by her admission. He looked, rather, a little bit amused. Though surprised, she was immensely relieved. Perhaps if he could forgive her this, they would not have to part in anger.

"Oh, well, I guess I should have known it was hopeless. I'm..." She smiled wryly. "I'm not a very good liar. I'm not subtle enough, I suppose. I'm kind of...well, you put it best, didn't you? I'm not very good at planning ahead."

"No," he agreed equably. "No, you're not."

She managed another small smile. "You don't *have* to agree with everything so quickly, you know. You could pretend to be surprised, just to help me save face."

"Sorry," he said. "But when you're right, you're right. And besides, Mrs. H. already told me everything that happened with Ted and Sheila—I suspect she had her ear to the door during the whole reconciliation scene. She certainly knew a lot of morbid details, like the fact that Ted actually allows Sheila to call him Neddie."

Melanie laughed. "Good heavens. Even I hadn't heard that."

Clay chuckled. "Well, Mrs. H. is a pro at this, as I believe you already know. I heard all about your telephone call last night, which set up the surprise encounter. And I met the happy couple myself on the way in just now—they were making a beeline to a justice of the peace, I suspect."

She nodded, glad for once that Mrs. H. was an incurable eavesdropper. It made things much easier—she had so little left to explain.

"They did seem happy, didn't they?" She remembered how Sheila had hugged her, how both of them had tears in their eyes as Melanie had slipped the diamond off her finger and handed it to Ted. It fitted Sheila so much better, and Melanie's own hand had felt suddenly light and free. "It was thrilling. Apparently, ever since their breakup a year ago, they've both been suffering, longing to patch it up, but they were both too proud to make the first move."

Clay eyed her carefully. "So you made the first move for them," he said. "That was very unselfish of you."

She waved that away. "Oh, no," she said, reluctant to be complimented. "Honestly, it *really* wasn't. Ted said that, too. He felt rotten about letting me down, but I wasn't going to be able to go through with the marriage anyhow. I guess I had already begun to see that it couldn't possibly work."

He spoke carefully. "Still, playing matchmaker for them might well have cost you over twelve million dollars. And what about the ruby? What about the house?"

She sighed, looking around her at the honeyed room. "Yes, the house. Actually that's the only part I regret. Ted really did need Cartouche Court, you know. You should have seen his plans, Clay. He wants to open a private school for disabled boys. It's a shame I won't be able to give him the chance.''

''And are you so sure you won't?'' Clay's voice sounded determinedly neutral. ''Dillard has agreed to take over the probate of the estate. Perhaps he'll decide in your favor, and Cartouche Court will be yours to do with as you please.''

''Oh, Clay,'' she said, grinning in spite of herself, ''we both know it would take a blind man to mistake me for a wise woman—and I don't think Mr. Dillard is blind.''

Clay let one corner of his mouth rise. ''He certainly didn't appear to be this afternoon. He couldn't quite take his eyes off you.''

She shook her head ruefully. ''If that's true, it must have been the allure of Ms. Daveed's wedding dress. Just wait till he sees what I look like in my beauty mask and thumbscrews.''

He chuckled. ''To tell you the truth, I'd rather he didn't.''

She sighed again. ''Besides, Clay, it doesn't really matter anymore. As difficult as it may be to believe after all we've been through, I don't even want the money now.''

He gazed at her steadily. ''You don't?''

''No, I really don't.'' She plucked thoughtfully at the flowing golden silk of the beautiful dress she wore, settling it around her knees in swirling folds of fabric. ''The one thing I've discovered from all this is that it's hopeless to try to be something you aren't. I guess I'm tired of trying to conform to some mold, some lawyer's stereotype of what a mature young woman should be.''

He knitted his brows and smiled quizzically. ''*Some lawyer*?''

She flushed. God, would she *never* learn the art of tactfully monitoring her words? ''You know what I mean. I know I'm not the kind of woman you admire, the kind you'd entrust with Joshua's millions. I tried to be—God knows I would have liked to earn your...admiration.'' She was still adjusting the dress, hardly able to meet his gaze for fear he'd see the heartbreak behind her eyes.

She tried to adopt a lighter tone. ''But I guess I'm stuck being me. And now that it's all over, I just want to get back to my real life—back to work, back to helping Nick grow up.

We don't need money—you were right about that all along. We just need to love each other. For a while, I think I forgot how much power love really has."

Clay's voice was serious. "Are you absolutely certain about this, Melanie? Would you be willing to sign away your claim to the inheritance?"

She finally looked up. Naturally he was still primarily concerned about the money—and about his liability as executor. Why should that knowledge sting? Had she actually allowed herself to hope that he had started to think of her as a person—as a woman—rather than as a "contingent beneficiary"?

"Of course," she said, trying not to let her disappointment show in her voice. "You can tell the National Research Foundation they just won the lottery."

But Clay was shaking his head. "No, they haven't," he said cryptically. "Quite the opposite, in fact."

She frowned. What on earth did that mean?

With a smile, he leaned back, digging in his pants pocket with one hand and pulling out a large, black velvet box. "Back in my office," he said conversationally, "I have a piece of paper, a sort of codicil to your uncle's will. It wasn't presented for probate because it wouldn't take effect unless you decided you didn't want to try to claim your inheritance."

She was so confused she felt furrows forming between her brows. "What does this codicil say?"

"It says that, if ever Miss Melanie Browning should relinquish all interest in her uncle's estate, Joshua Browning's executor is at that moment required to pronounce her fit to inherit. Wisdom to see that money is not worth fighting for, he said, is wisdom enough to handle it well."

She was shaking her head even while he was speaking. "*Joshua* said those words?" She couldn't have been more astonished. Joshua had always believed that money *was* worth fighting for. Worth dying for, even. It was the Browning tradition. He must have changed far more than she realized. "But what," she asked, "what does that really mean in practical terms?"

Clay opened the velvet box. In it lay the Romeo Ruby, a glowing heart of flawless stone that captured the sunlight and threw it out again in sparks of honey rose and fire. He held it out to her, smiling. "It means you've said the magic word, Melanie. It means the National Research Foundation directors will be weeping into their coffee cups tomorrow morning. It means you're a very rich young woman."

She felt reality faltering. This simply didn't make any sense at all. "But I don't want it!" she protested, holding up her hand as if she could block the box from reaching her. "I honestly, truly, don't want it."

"I know," he said, grinning, laying the box on her lap. "But it's yours. Isn't that just like your uncle? Perverse to the bitter end."

She scowled down at the ruby. "Well, do I have to accept it? Can't the primary beneficiary defer to the secondary beneficiaries, or some such gobbledygook?" She flipped the box shut and set it on the table behind them, somewhere among all the handcuffs. Where it belonged, she thought acidly, relishing the small poetic justice. She glared at Clay. "You're a big-shot lawyer. You wrote the will. You must know how to get around it."

He looked her over slowly. "Yes," he said. "I suppose a lawyer, Dillard, perhaps, could arrange something like that, if you really wanted it. And it might, after all, make things a little less complicated."

"Things?" She mistrusted his tone. She knew that tone, that bland innocence that hid a world of mischief. But it was one of the things she loved about him, this capacity for laughing just slightly at the world, and at himself. "What things?"

Was it a trick of the sunset, or were his brown eyes twinkling? "Well, for one thing, it might help protect my reputation."

"How so?"

"It would spare me from accusations of being a gigolo. It won't do my law practice any good if people believe I'm just the latest in a long line of Romeos to ask a rich Browning heiress to marry him."

She stared at him. "To ask a Browning heiress to *what*?"

"To marry him," he repeated slowly, as if he understood that her brain had suddenly ceased to function. He touched her shoulder lightly with his forefinger, sending ripples of shivering sunlight through her. "You know, to live with him as man and wife, for richer, for poorer, in sickness and in health. You're familiar with the words, I'm sure. You've even said them once or twice.''

"Once," she insisted, finding it easier to correct his nonsense than to deal with the more serious implications. She didn't even dare to believe it *was* serious. "But I didn't mean them then. I was only sixteen, you know. And I'd never been in love." She swallowed. "I didn't even know what love was."

"What about now?" He was leaning very close. She noticed with a wonderful, terrible, sinking sensation that his beautiful brown eyes were filled with sunshine flecks. Oh, how she loved his eyes.... "Do you know what love is now, Melanie?"

"Yes," she said quietly. "Yes, I honestly think I do."

Smiling, he reached out and pulled her toward him. Silk whispered as it dragged across leather, rustled as it folded against the white cotton of his shirt.

"I thought you might," he said softly, ducking to kiss the bare skin at her throat. "But still...I'm not sure you know enough." He smiled up at her through thick sable lashes. "This kind of love is different. I didn't know about it myself until I met you."

She listened to her heart beating wildly against her throat. "Different? How?"

"Well," he said, addressing his lips again to her neck, her collarbone, her shoulder. "It's dangerous. It's the kind of love that can make a very respectable lawyer dream every night of making forbidden love to his client. And it's powerful. It's the kind of love that makes a lifelong square, a self-satisfied stuffed shirt, want to spend the rest of his life whirling about on an emotional roller coaster."

"Oh, my," she said softly, running her fingers through the thick velvet of his hair. "That is extreme."

"Yes, I'm just about done for, I think," he said complacently, sliding his feet up onto the sofa and deftly arranging her so that she lay nearly on top of him, their legs entwined, her head in the crook of his shoulder. White silk spilled over them and trailed onto the floor. "I'll probably have to give up the law. I'm so desperately in love with you I can't think straight." His hands had found her back and were caressing the bare skin where the low-cut wedding dress left her vulnerable and exposed. She felt him make his way toward the soft velvet bow. "I will never again be able to live without your laughter, without your smiles, without your completely charming and utterly impractical way of looking at the world."

She could hardly speak. "But...you know I drive you crazy," she whispered.

"Yes, you do," he agreed happily. "You drive me absolutely out of my mind. And I've discovered that it's a very sexy place to be."

"Have you forgotten how stubborn I am? I have very poor impulse control."

"Of course I haven't forgotten." He tugged on the bow. She felt it fall apart. "It may be what I love most about you."

"And remember, I'm quite dangerous." Her whole body was beginning to tremble as his fingers worked their magic. "Wedding dresses don't come equipped with weapons, but I'm usually armed, you know."

"Why should I worry about that? I'm already your prisoner," he said huskily. "You know you captured my heart at swordpoint the first day I met you."

The last buttons of her gown slipped open. As she felt cool air tease along her back, which was now bare from neck to hip, she drew back. "We must be mad." She glanced nervously toward the door. "Someone might come in. Where are the others?"

"Anywhere but here," he assured her. "I told them all I would personally strangle the first fool who dares to knock on that door."

"Oh, dear." She sighed, already distracted by the feel of his palms on her bare arms as he eased them free of the soft silk. "Apparently it's catching. You're starting to sound as bloodthirsty as I am."

"Besides," he said, sliding the gown over her hips, "the doors are locked. You and I are alone, my love...."

But the words were premature. As Clay took the yards of white silk and tossed them to the floor, a salacious voice suddenly whistled. "Oooh, sweet!" Copernicus was clearly watching from his cage. "Lookin' *good*!"

Clay swore, his vocabulary every bit as impressive as the

parrot's. He didn't let go of Melanie, but with his free arm he balled up the wedding dress and tossed it behind him, arcing it gracefully over his head toward Copernicus. It landed with a soft whoosh on the birdcage, its full skirts cascading down on all sides.

"Well, damn," the parrot began. "What the he—"

Melanie and Clay looked at each other, grinning. "*Copernicus*," they commanded in perfect unison, "*shut up!*"

And for once in his life, Copernicus did.

MILLS & BOON®

Next Month's Romance Titles

♡

Each month you can choose from a wide variety of romance novels from Mills & Boon®. Below are the new titles to look out for next month from the Presents™ and Enchanted™ series.

Presents™

PACIFIC HEAT	Anne Mather
THE BRIDAL BED	Helen Bianchin
THE YULETIDE CHILD	Charlotte Lamb
MISTLETOE MISTRESS	Helen Brooks
A CHRISTMAS SEDUCTION	Amanda Browning
THE THIRTY-DAY SEDUCTION	Kay Thorpe
FIANCÉE BY MISTAKE	Kate Walker
A NICE GIRL LIKE YOU	Alexandra Sellers

Enchanted™

FIANCÉ FOR CHRISTMAS	Catherine George
THE HUSBAND PROJECT	Leigh Michaels
COMING HOME FOR CHRISTMAS	Laura Martin
THE BACHELOR AND THE BABIES	Heather MacAllister
THE NUTCRACKER PRINCE	Rebecca Winters
FATHER BY MARRIAGE	Suzanne Carey
THE BILLIONAIRE'S BABY CHASE	Valerie Parv
ROMANTICS ANONYMOUS	Lauryn Chandler

On sale from 4th December 1998

H1 9811

Available at most branches of WH Smith, Tesco, Asda, Martins, Borders and all good paperback bookshops

CHRISTMAS

Affairs

MORE THAN JUST KISSES UNDER THE MISTLETOE...

Enjoy three sparkling seasonal romances by your
favourite authors from

MILLS & BOON®
Presents™

HELEN BIANCHIN
For Anique, the season of goodwill has become...
The Seduction Season

SANDRA MARTON
Can Santa weave a spot of Christmas magic for Nick
and Holly in... *A Miracle on Christmas Eve?*

SHARON KENDRICK
Will Aleck and Clemmie have a... *Yuletide Reunion?*

MILLS & BOON®

Makes any time special™

Available from 6th November 1998

Your Special Christmas Gift

Three romance novels from Mills & Boon® to
unwind with at your leisure—
and a luxurious Le Jardin bath gelée to pamper
you and gently wash your cares away.

for just £5.99

Featuring
Carole Mortimer—Married by Christmas
Betty Neels—A Winter Love Story
Jo Leigh—One Wicked Night

MILLS & BOON®

Makes your Christmas time special

Available from 23rd October 1998

4 FREE

books and a surprise gift!

We would like to take this opportunity to thank you for reading this Mills & Boon® book by offering you the chance to take FOUR more specially selected titles from the Presents™ series absolutely FREE! We're also making this offer to introduce you to the benefits of the Reader Service™—

- ★ FREE home delivery
- ★ FREE gifts and competitions
- ★ FREE monthly Newsletter
- ★ Books available before they're in the shops
- ★ Exclusive Reader Service discounts

Accepting these FREE books and gift places you under no obligation to buy, you may cancel at any time, even after receiving your free shipment. Simply complete your details below and return the entire page to the address below. *You don't even need a stamp!*

YES! Please send me 4 free Presents books and a surprise gift. I understand that unless you hear from me, I will receive 6 superb new titles every month for just £2.30 each, postage and packing free. I am under no obligation to purchase any books and may cancel my subscription at any time. The free books and gift will be mine to keep in any case.

P8YE

Ms/Mrs/Miss/Mr.................................Initials ....
BLOCK CAPITALS PLEASE

Surname ....

Address ....

....

....Postcode...............................

Send this whole page to:
THE READER SERVICE, FREEPOST, CROYDON, CR9 3WZ
(Eire readers please send coupon to: P.O. BOX 4546, DUBLIN 24.)

Offer not valid to current Reader Service subscribers to this series. We reserve the right to refuse an application and applicants must be aged 18 years or over. Only one application per household. Terms and prices subject to change without notice. Offer expires 31st May 1999. As a result of this application, you may receive further offers from Harlequin Mills & Boon and other carefully selected companies. If you would prefer not to share in this opportunity please write to The Data Manager, P.O. Box 236, Croydon, Surrey CR9 3RU.

Mills & Boon Presents is being used as a trademark.

MILLS & BOON®

Makes any time special

Enjoy a romantic novel from Mills & Boon®

Presents™ *Enchanted™* *Temptation*

Historical Romance™ *Medical Romance*